Fox Tales

Fox Tales

Edited by
Jennifer Taylor

Illustrated by Trevor Newton

RED FOX

A Red Fox Book
Published by Random Century Children's Books
20 Vauxhall Bridge Road, London SW1V 2SA

A division of the Random Century Group
London Melbourne Sydney Auckland
Johannesburg and agencies throughout the world

First published by Red Fox 1992

Set in Baskerville
by JH Graphics Ltd, Reading

Printed and bound in Great Britain by
Cox & Wyman Ltd, Reading, Berks

ISBN 0 09 997530 0

Contents

For Anna Louise,
who still likes foxes,
although her hens
Mathilda and Henrietta
were carried off
one winter's night
by a Hampshire fox

Introduction

I have always liked foxes, who seem to me to shine out as highly attractive and intelligent animals. They take chickens, of course, but then put your average, friendly household cat on a diet (no Whiskas for a week) and give him opportunity (a bunch of dozy sparrows), and see what a meal he makes of them. 'Naughty pussy', the cat will be ticked off; foxes are shot and hunted, and treated as vermin.

Foxes have had a reputation for cunning for centuries (even in pre-Biblical times), and since they exist in every European country, as well as Russia, Japan, North America and parts of Asia and Australia, it is not surprising that foxes crop up in the folk tales of many countries. You can sometimes see wood carvings in medieval cathedrals of the fox and the grapes, as in Aesop's fable, or the fox preaching to the geese.

Ironically, foxes have now to some extent sought refuge in towns. Cities such as Bristol and Oxford, and also some suburbs of London, have a considerable fox population. They are generally safer there because town dwellers tend to think of them as 'cute'. Some foxes 'commute' — living in the country-side but going into town at night to raid bird tables and dustbins. Have you ever seen a fox slinking along a city street late at night?

Some of the royalties from this book will go to St Tiggy-winkles Wildlife Hospital Trust, near Aylesbury, which takes in something like 8000 sick and injured animals a year, includ-ing sparrows, swans, deer, badgers and hedgehogs, as well as hundreds of foxes which have either been caught in snares, shot or hit by cars. The aim is of course to get the animals back into the wild as soon as possible.

You can join 'Tiggy's Club', and receive free fact sheets, a badge and a magazine. You can also sponsor an animal, from £10 for a hedgehog to £30 for a fox.

The hospital is run by Les Stocker and his wife, Sue, who says that foxes are her favourite animals of all. 'They are clean and beautiful. They should be seen as an asset, the farmer's best friend, since they take pests such as mice and rats. They should be king of our animals.'

The fox's quickwitted adaptability was contrasted several centuries ago with the hedgehog's slow, steadfast concentration, and compared to similar human types. So which are you in character, a fox or a hedgehog?

Jennifer Taylor

Sanctuary

from *Who Ever Heard of a Vegetarian Fox?*

by Rosalind Kerven

Foxes are indeed no vegetarians. They do like their rations of meat. But they will in fact eat whatever is available, from blackberries and grapes — as in Aesop's famous fable — to worms and half empty containers from take-away shops.

In this extract from Rosalind Kerven's book, set in the country, Sarah and her older sister Caroline, who care passionately about animals, have just freed a fox caught in a trap set by the local gamekeeper, and taken him to Ian, who runs a wildlife sanctuary . . . and is none other than the gamekeeper's son.

'Right. Just put him down inside. I'll take over now.'

They slipped the stretcher gently into the cage.

Ian crawled in, loosened the bundle and pulled the covers off the fox. It lolled on the ground, its eyes glazed, its jaws snapping angrily, helplessly.

Ian muttered softly to it under his breath. He reached for a thick stick and pushed it into its half-open mouth as if he were giving a bone to a dog. The fox sank its teeth into it.

'Hey, Sarah — see that tap in the corner?'

'Yes.'

'There's some tin bowls by it. Fill us one with water. Bring it here. And there's a box of clean rags in that empty cage by the back door. It's open. Bring us a handful.'

She hesitated.

'*Quickly.*'

She got what he needed. Ian crouched over the fox, cleaning its bad leg. The shock of cold water on the wound seemed to make the animal swoon: its eyes closed and the stick fell from its jaws. Ian seized the opportunity to work more firmly.

'You seem to know what you're doing,' remarked Caroline; but she couldn't keep the resentment out of her voice.

Ian glanced up at her. 'It's a nasty one this. Reckon the rot's already set in — gangrene maybe.'

'*Please*, Ian,' said Sarah, 'do everything you can to try and save him.'

He gave an impatient grunt. 'Pity him or his mate didn't have as much sympathy as you when they went scrounging after eggs last spring. Scrunched up a dozen nests, they did — and managed to kill a couple of hen pheasants too, for the hell of it.'

He finished cleaning the wound, tore off some fresh strips of rag, and used them to bind the stick to the fox's leg like a splint.

'Right, best be out of the way now.' He crawled backwards out of the cage. 'Fetch us a clean bowl of water for him to drink — and pour this one down that drain.'

Sarah ran about, doing everything he asked. He put the clean water inside, then snapped the cage door shut.

The fox lay inside, shivering, eyes half opening, drifting in and out of consciousness. Ian watched it critically.

'He'll take some nursing, he will — and some feeding up.' He gave Sarah a friendly slap across the shoulders and flashed a mirthless smile at Caroline. 'Seeing as you rescued him and brought him here, he's like your charge, OK? So how's about you take care of bringing him his food?'

'*Us?*' said Sarah.

'How do you feed the other animals you keep here?' asked Caroline.

'Well, they're mostly small things like birds and rabbits and bats, so they're no trouble: worms, corn, grass, flies' — he winked at Sarah — 'that sort of thing. But foxes are different now. Meat eaters, they are.'

'Can't you give him tinned dog food?' suggested Sarah.

'Yeah, I *could*,' said Ian. He stared at Caroline straight in the eye. 'But you heard what Dad said about feeding him: I can't really see him agreeing to share his best gundogs' dinner with Arch Enemy Number One — can you?'

'So — what then?' said Sarah.

'You'll have to bring things for him — like nice juicy rabbits.'

'Rabbits?' cried Sarah. 'You want *us* to catch rabbits?'

'Aye,' said Ian calmly.

'But we can't possibly! We couldn't go round killing animals. Not . . . not even for *him*. It's against everything we believe in. Isn't there something else he could have?'

Ian shook his head solemnly.

'Nope. It's fresh meat he needs. I mean — who ever heard of a vegetarian fox?'

The Fox and the Grapes

The original case of sour grapes.

by Aesop

One day a fox, who was hot and tired and very thirsty, saw
some bunches of ripe juicy grapes growing on a vine high out
of reach. How he wanted those grapes! He tried to get at them
by standing on tiptoe and stretching, but they were still out of
reach. This made him want them more than ever. So he began
to jump up as high as he could, but they were still *just* out of
reach. At last he gave up, tired and cross, and walked away as
though he couldn't care less.

'I didn't really want them,' he said. 'They looked very sour.'
But he knew they weren't, of course.

The Fox's Foray

from *English Fairy Tales*

by Joseph Jacobs

The fox went out, one still, clear night,
And he prayed the moon to give him light,
For he'd a long way to travel that night,
  Before he got back to his den-o!

The fox when he came to yonder stile,
He lifted his lugs and he listened a while!
'Oh, ho!' said the fox, 'it's but a short mile
  From this unto yonder wee town, e-ho!'

And first he arrived at a farmer's yard,
Where the ducks and geese declared it was hard,
That their nerves should be shaken and their rest should
    be marred
  By the visits of Mister Fox-o!

The fox when he came to the farmer's gate,
Who should he see but the farmer's drake;
'I love you well for your master's sake,
  And long to be picking your bones, e-ho!'

The grey goose she ran round the hay-stack,
'Oh, ho!' said the fox, 'you are very fat;
You'll grease my beard and ride on my back
   From this into yonder wee town, e-ho!'

Then he took the grey goose by her sleeve,
And said: 'Madam Grey Goose, by your leave
I'll take you away without reprieve,
   And carry you back to my den-o!'

And he seized the black duck by the neck,
And slung him all across his back,
The black duck cried out 'quack, quack, quack',
   With his legs all dangling down-o!

Old Mother Wiggle-Waggle hopped out of bed,
Out of the window she popped her old head;
'Oh! husband, oh! husband, the grey goose is gone,
   And the fox is off to his den, oh!'

Then the old man got up in his red cap,
And swore he would catch the fox in a trap;
But the fox was too cunning, and gave him the slip,
   And ran through the town, the town, oh!

When he got to the top of the hill,
He blew his trumpet both loud and shrill,
For joy that he was safe and sound
   Through the town, oh!

But at last he arrived at his home again,
To his dear little foxes, eight, nine, ten,
Says he 'You're in luck, here's a fine fat duck
  With his legs all dangling down-o!'

So he sat down together with his hungry wife,
And they did very well without fork or knife,
They never ate a better duck in all their life,
  And the little ones picked the bones-o!

Sleepy fox has seldom feathered breakfasts.
                     Old English Proverb

Clever Mr Fox

from *Fantastic Mr Fox*

by Roald Dahl

In Roald Dahl's celebrated tale, Mr Fox and his family are trapped in their earth under a hill while farmers Boggis, Bunce and Bean, whose farms are nearby, stand watch outside with their guns. But clever Mr Fox has a plan . . .

'This time we must go in a very special direction,' said Mr Fox, pointing sideways and downward.

So he and his four children started to dig once again. The work went much more slowly now. Yet they kept at it with great courage, and little by little the tunnel began to grow.

'Dad, I wish you would tell us *where* we are going,' said one of the children.

'I dare not do that,' said Mr Fox, 'because this place I am *hoping* to get to is so *marvellous* that if I described it to you now you would go crazy with excitement. And then, if we failed to get there (which is very possible), you would die of disappointment. I don't want to raise your hopes too much, my darlings.'

For a long, long time they kept on digging. For how long they did not know, because there were no days and no nights down there in the murky tunnel. But at last Mr Fox gave the order to stop. 'I think,' he said, 'we had better take a peep upstairs now and see where we are. I know where I *want* to be, but I can't possibly be sure we're anywhere near it.'

Slowly, wearily, the foxes began to slope the tunnel up towards the surface. Up and up it went . . . until suddenly they came to something hard above their heads and they couldn't go up any further. Mr Fox reached up to examine this hard thing. 'It's wood!' he whispered. 'Wooden planks!'

'What does that mean, Dad?'

'It means, unless I am very much mistaken, that we are right underneath somebody's house,' whispered Mr Fox. 'Be quiet now while I take a peek.'

Carefully, Mr Fox began pushing up one of the floorboards. The board creaked most terribly and they all ducked down, waiting for something awful to happen. Nothing did. So Mr Fox pushed up a second board. And then, very very cautiously, he poked his head up through the gap. He let out a shriek of excitement.

'I've done it!' he yelled. 'I've done it *first time!* I've done it! I've *done it!'* He pulled himself up through the gap in the floor and started prancing and dancing with joy. 'Come on up!' he sang out. 'Come up and see where you are, my darlings! What a sight for a hungry fox! Hallelujah! Hooray! Hooray!'

The four Small Foxes scrambled up out of the tunnel and what a fantastic sight it was that now met their eyes! They were in a huge shed and the whole place was teeming with chickens. There were white chickens and brown chickens and black chickens by the thousand!

'Boggis's Chicken House Number One!' cried Mr Fox. 'It's exactly what I was aiming at! I hit it slap in the middle! First time! Isn't that fantastic! *And*, if I may say so, rather clever!'

The Small Foxes went wild with excitement. They started running around in all directions, chasing the stupid chickens.

'Wait!' ordered Mr Fox. 'Don't lose your heads! Stand back!

Calm down! Let's do this properly! First of all, everyone have
a drink of water!'

They all ran over to the chickens' drinking-trough and lapped
up the lovely cool water. Then Mr Fox chose three of the
plumpest hens, and with a clever flick of his jaws he killed them
instantly.

'Back to the tunnel!' he ordered. 'Come on! No fooling
around! The quicker you move, the quicker you shall have
something to eat!'

One after another, they climbed down through the hole in
the floor and soon they were all standing once again in the dark
tunnel. Mr Fox reached up and pulled the floorboards back into
place. He did this with great care. He did it so that no one could
tell they had ever been moved.

'My son,' he said, giving the three plump hens to the biggest
of his four small children, 'run back with these to your mother.
Tell her to prepare a feast. Tell her the rest of us will be along
in a jiffy, as soon as we have made a few other little
arrangements.'

When the fox preaches, then beware your geese.
                              Old English Proverb

Frozen Chickens

from Sauce for the Fox

by Brian Morse

It's tomato sauce, to be precise, that Mr Fox, in Brian Morse's amusing tale, has developed a taste for. Having recently moved to town, he finds that worms and insects are harder to come by. So when a cat invites him into his house to help him raid the kitchen, Mr Fox goes with him against his better instincts. He has already successfully opened the fridge door, enabling the cat to scoff a bowl of pilchards, but what about those chickens the cat promised him? The cat indicates the freezer, which is harder to open.

He turned away from the window. He was leaving, giving the whole thing up as a bad job. Then he had an idea. It was probably the most brilliant idea in the history of foxes.

He got to work straightaway. He deliberately pushed the chair over. The cat opened an eye, sniggered, then dozed off again. Mr Fox almost nipped its rump, he felt so happy.

He got the chair right, balanced one leg on his snout, lifted it and hooked it through the freezer handle. If only his wife were here to watch! And the cubs! He was going to *lever* the freezer open! He had become an inventor! He pushed on the back of

the chair with all his might. It worked! The door snapped open!
Cold air and frosty mist curled out towards him.

He'd done it! Mr Fox took his weight off the chair. The
freezer door banged to again.

Mr Fox kept calm. He put his weight on the chair again.
When the freezer door opened he didn't let go.

However, only the scent of ice and snow came out, no smells
of food. He poked his snout in. Cub! It was cold! A wild
thought went through his mind — this was where winter disappeared to in spring. He must get this over quickly. He didn't
want winter escaping into the garden.

The freezer was bursting with cold, scentless polythene
packets and plastic boxes. Many of them were covered with a
rime of frost. Mr Fox stepped back in dismay. The food was
hibernating! Mrs Fox wouldn't eat food like this! She'd murder
him first!

'You trickster! You low-down thieving cheat!' He rounded on
the cat again. It opened a yellow eye.

'I see you've managed it, fox. Well done! Congratulations.'

'You brought me here on false pretences.'

'Grab a chicken. She put several in last week.'

'Everything's rock-solid.'

'Then thaw them out. How ignorant you are, fox! What did
you expect — a hen trotting out squawking "Eat me!"? A couple
of hours in the sun and they'll be perfect. Did you know they
even wrap up the giblets in the middle to save you searching?'

'Really?' Mr Fox still felt doubtful.

'Go on, fox. Take them, but just get out before my woman
comes back. She won't like you at all. People don't like foxes.
I can't imagine why.'

Mr Fox allowed himself a smile. Three days without hunting. No getting up with the early bird. He could turn over and
go back to sleep instead of leaping out of the den. He nudged
the packages in the freezer about.

A shapeless package fell out and landed on his front paws.

The vixen lost no time, and started to throw the fish off the sledge into the road, one after the other, till the basket was empty. Then she jumped down.

When the old man got home, he rushed inside. 'I've brought you a fur collar for your coat,' he said to the old woman. 'You've never seen such a fine one.'

'Where is it then?'

'At the back of the sledge, with the fish.'

But the old woman of course found neither fish nor fur collar, and she started scolding her husband. The old man moaned and groaned as he realized that the vixen had not been dead. But it was too late to do anything about that.

The vixen meanwhile had gathered up in a heap all the fish she had thrown out on to the road, and settled down to a feast by the roadside.

A grey wolf was passing that way. 'Good evening, sister,' he greeter her.

'Good evening, brother!'

'Give me the fish,' said the wolf.

'Go and catch your own — then you can have as much as you want,' said the little vixen.

'I don't know how.'

'Then do as I did, brother: go down to the river, step on to the ice and stick your tail through a hole in it — then sit there saying over and over:

> "Fish, large and small, come and bite,
> Fish, large and small, come and bite!"

'This will make the fish come and hang on to your tail. But you must be prepared to sit there for a long time, otherwise you won't catch a thing.'

So the wolf went down to the river, stuck his tail into the water, and started repeating, over and over, what the vixen had told him to say.

The vixen meanwhile padded around in the background wailing softly to herself:

Little Sister Vixen
and the Wolf

by Alexander Afanasiev

Foxes, who feature prominently in Russian animal folk tales as smooth-tongued deceivers, are always portrayed as vixens, and since the Russian for 'fox' is 'lissa', they are often given the name Liza.

In this tale collected by Afanasiev — the Russian equivalent of the Grimm brothers in the nineteenth century — the object of her deception, as in the folk tales of so many other countries, is the dim-witted grey wolf.

An old peasant lived with his old wife. One cold winter's day he said to her: 'While you're making the dough for pies, old woman, I'll harness the sledge and go down to the river, and bring back some fish for our supper.'

He indeed caught a lot of fish, and set off for home at dusk. As the sledge trundled along, he saw a vixen lying in the middle of the road, curled up in a ball.

The old man went up to the vixen, and prodded her gently with a stick. But she did not move, and lay as though dead. 'The fur will make a fine present for the old lady,' thought the old man with glee. So he picked up the vixen, placed her next to the basket of fish, and walked on in front.

'Shine, shine, stars in the sky,
Freeze, freeze the tail in the ice.'

'What's that you're saying, sister vixen?'

'I'm trying to help you,' said the little mischief-maker, but she kept on repeating the words: 'Freeze, freeze the tail in the ice.'

The wolf sat, and sat; he sat there the whole night long, and his tail froze hard. It was winter, remember. When he tried to pull it out, it was stuck fast. 'That just shows how many fish I've caught,' he thought.

When morning came, he saw old women coming down to the river with their buckets for water. As soon as they saw him they shouted: 'Wolf, wolf! Beat him, beat him!'

They ran up and gave him a drubbing with whatever they had to hand. The wolf tried to jump this way and that to avoid the blows, and he jumped up so high that he left his tail behind. As he ran off as fast as his legs would carry him, he thought of the vixen who had tricked him. 'I'll pay you back, sister,' he said.

But the little vixen, not satisfied with her night's work, wanted to go one better. She dashed into a hut where some old women were making pancakes, and plunged her head into the tub of batter. She got it all over herself and ran off.

She saw the wolf coming towards her.

'That was some fishing lesson you gave me, sister. I was beaten black and blue!'

'Oh little brother wolf,' said the little vixen, 'you think you got a hard beating, do you? Well, I had a much harder one. Look, my brains were spilt, and I can hardly drag myself along.'

'If that's the truth, and I can see it is,' said the wolf, 'why, come and sit on my back, sister. I will carry you.'

So there was the little vixen, sitting on the wolf's back, singing quietly to herself:

'The beaten one is carrying the unbeaten one,
The beaten one is carrying the unbeaten one.'

'What's that you're saying, sister?'

'I'm saying, brother, that the beaten one is carrying the badly beaten one.'

'Quite so, sister, quite so!'

The fox that had lost its tail would persuade others out of theirs.

Proverb

The Fox's Earth

from *Little Foxes*

by Michael Morpurgo

The appeal of fox cubs as they tumble in mischievous play is obvious, and is enjoyed to the full in Michael Morpurgo's story. Billy, abandoned at birth, has lived with foster families all his life, and he finds a refuge in the wilderness by the canal, where he enjoys watching the birds and rabbits — and a family of foxes. But by the time we join the story the vixen has been killed, and several of the cubs have been gassed, and Billy, feeling desperately protective about the one surviving cub, has run away with him. A day and a night later find them in a wood.

You may think of Jack Russell terriers as nice little dogs, but foxes don't — they are traditional enemies. Terriers, or 'earth dogs', are great diggers and like nothing more than going down holes after foxes or badgers.

Morning came too soon for both of them. Bily had slept fitfully. Whichever side he chose to sleep on soon lost all feeling, and the pins and needles that followed were excrutiating. When he woke his neck was stiff and he was wet through and shivering with the cold. There were church bells ringing somewhere in the misty valley below him, and a cow lowing mournfully. A

persistent invisible pigeon called gently from above him in the
trees and a pair of circling buzzards mewed plaintively
overhead. Billy watched as a gang of raucous rooks moved in
to worry them.

The fox stiffened suddenly beside him at the bark of a dog.
Billy was not alarmed for it seemed to him to be harmless
enough and still far away. But then there was the murmur of
voices, a hooting laugh, and Billy was on his feet and running.
He followed the fox up the hillside and into the shelter of the
trees. As they ran in under the trees a gunshot blasted behind
them and the wood emptied itself noisily of every bird. The fox
ran on ahead the way he had gone the night before, and Billy
ran after him stumbling over the dead branches that the fox
leapt so easily. Another gunshot echoed along the valley behind
them. Billy did not know whether the shots were aimed at them.
The fox seemed to know and that was enough for him. Suddenly there were no more trees and Billy was out in the bright
sunlight and tearing downhill towards a stream. Beyond the
stream was a forest of conifer trees that climbed the hillside in
serried lines. There was cover in there. If they could reach the
trees Billy felt they had some chance. The fox loped across the
open field, hesitated at the stream but then bounded across and
up into the trees beyond. Billy splashed through the water after
him and plunged into the forest before turning to see if they
were being followed. He crouched in the shadows and watched.

Not fifty paces from them two men came out into the field,
each of them carrying a gun, a little Jack Russell terrier sniffing
the ground around them. 'I saw it,' said one of them. 'Big it was
and brown, I saw it, honest. Could've been a deer even. Gone
to cover in the Brigadier's wood. He's got dozens of them in
there. He won't notice if there's one missing, will he? Come on,
let's go in after him. It's worth a bit is a deer. Look, the dog's
after him, he's got his scent, I told you, I told you.' And sure
enough the little Jack Russell was bustling down through the
grass towards them, yapping as he came.

Upward was the only way to go. Billy dug his toes into the

soft earth and forced his legs to run. The fox needed no whistling on now. He trotted on easily in front, tongue hanging out. They could hear behind them that the hunters were in the woods too and that the yapping terrier was coming even closer. Billy ran now because the fox ran. He drove himself on, pounding the air with his arms, whispering through gritted teeth, 'Faster, faster, faster. Don't stop. Don't stop.'

With the forest behind them filling with excited voices they reached the forest path at the top of the hill. The fox immediately turned right as if he knew the way, so Billy followed him. Billy sensed that the fox was leading him somewhere, and he was far too tired to argue. When the fox left the track and bounded up the bank into more trees, Billy clambered after him.

It was a different forest now, with great tall oaks clinging dangerously to the hillside. Many had fallen, their roots ripped out leaving vast craters where young saplings were sprouting again. As they ran on and up, Billy saw the fox slowing. He was looking around him as he went, no longer intent it seemed on escape. The measured rhythm was gone from his stride and Billy found himself running alongside him, even ahead of him sometimes. Fatigue overcame Billy now as he laboured on, fatigue brought on by the knowledge that he had not thrown off their pursuers. Below in the woods they could hear them crashing through the undergrowth and always that shrill incessant yapping that was leading the hunters inexorably towards them.

The fox had paused by one of the craters, and quite suddenly vanished among the roots. Billy whistled for him but the fox did not reappear, so Billy went down into the crater after him. The earth still clung to the roots that towered now over Billy, an earth wall of twisted roots, and at the root of it a hole that must have been torn out of the hillside when the tree fell. It seemed to lead in behind the wall of roots, and at the mouth of the hole he saw the white muzzle of the fox. Billy had no idea how big the hole might be inside, but the hunters were so close now that there was no time for debate. He thrust himself into the hole, arms and head first, but his shoulders stuck fast. He kicked out furiously with his legs and groped in the dark for something on which he could haul himself in, and he found it, a gnarled root that was strong enough to take all his weight. Once inside he looked for the fox and found two eyes staring back at him out of the dark. He gathered the fox to him and crawled to the back of the earth cave and waited. Whatever happened he would never allow the fox to be taken from him.

The terrier came straight to the hole and would have come in after them had not Billy hurled a clod of earth and stones at his snarling snout. It took a broadside to drive him away and he backed off, yelping in surprise. Billy crouched in the dark with the fox breathing heavily against him, and they heard the hunters' voices as they toiled up the hillside towards the dog that stood quivering and barking at the bottom of the crater.

'Ain't no deer down there. You and your deer, Jack. Run me ruddy legs off I did, and for what?' said one of them. 'Rabbits, that's all there is in there. Came all this way for a ruddy rabbit we did. Lost the scent, didn't he, the useless mutt.'

'He's after something though isn't he?' said another voice. 'There's a hole down there, see? Big enough for a fox, that is. P'raps it was a fox after all, p'raps he's after a fox. Let's put him in there and see, eh? We came all this way, didn't we? Worth a try.' And Billy heard them slithering down into the crater. He grabbed the biggest stone he could find from the floor of the cave and watched for the terrier's nose to appear again. But instead of the dog it was a face they saw, a woolly head of ginger hair and a red face. 'Pitch black in there, can't see a thing. Give me the dog. If anything's in there he'll soon bring it out. You'll see.'

But nothing would persuade the terrier to put its nose to the hole again. More than once they dragged the wretched animal choking to the mouth of the hole and held it there, pushing it from behind, but the dog dug its front feet into the ground obstinately and backed out yelping just as soon as they let go of his collar. Billy held his fire and hoped.

'There's something in there, got to be. Got to be something in there to make the dog turn tail.'

'He's a useless mutt, Jack, like I said. You should get yourself a proper dog. Yellow as a buttercup he is.'

'Look, if he's frightened, then he's frightened of something, right? So there's got to be something down there, hasn't there? Now if he won't go in after it and drag it out, then we've got to persuade whatever's in there to come out, haven't we?'

'Yeah, but how're we gonna do that, Jack?'

'I'm coming to that. First we got to be sure there isn't another way out of there. We got to block off any other way out. So you get round the other side of that old root and if you find another hole, kick it in so's he can't get out. Then we got him trapped, see?'

Billy listened to the scrambling feet clambering about outside. 'Nothing here,' came a voice from behind the earth wall at the back of the cave. Under Billy's arm the fox licked his lips, gathered his tongue in and listened for a moment, then began to pant in short sharp bursts, every so often pausing to listen again. 'Hey, I think I can hear something. I can, I can. There's breathing inside there.' Billy clasped his hand over the fox's snout to close it and stroked his ears gently to calm him down. 'There's something in there, Jack, I heard it, clear as day. I heard it.'

'If there's something inside there, then it won't want to be there for long. Got a little surprise for it, a nice little surprise. Come back here, and give me a hand. A few twigs and dry leaves — 's all we need.' And Billy heard them climbing up out of the crater sending little avalanches of earth and stones tumbling down behind them, a few of them finding their way into the mouth of the cave.

When the voices were far enough away Billy crawled forward to take a look. There was just a chance he thought they might be able to escape before the hunters came back. He could not think why they had gone off to gather twigs and leaves, but whatever it was he did not want to be trapped in that cave when the hunters came back again. When he was sure it was all clear he pushed the fox out in front of him and prepared to follow him out. But the fox seemed reluctant to go and struggled to turn round. As Billy pushed him again, there was a hideous growl and suddenly the terrier was there in front of them, stocky on its four little legs, its lips curled back over its teeth that snapped out its machine-gun rattle of a bark. The fox did not hesitate, but was back through the hole and at the back of the cave before Billy could hurl the stone he still held in his hand. He missed, but it was enough to persuade the terrier to retreat again while he gathered some more ammunition. And then the hunters were coming back, slithering down the slope and laughing as they came.

'All talk, that dog of yours, Jack, all mouth he is.'

'This'll do the trick, you'll see. Just put it down by the hole there. That's it, a nice pile — only the dry stuff mind you. Don't want anything wet. Now give us that bit of cord you got holding your trousers up.'

'But they'll fall down.'

'Don't matter about that. Who's to see? Come on, give it here. Plenty more of it back at the farm. Can't get a fire lit without it can we? And it's got to be a good fire. Then we put the leaves on it and push it down that hole and whatever's in there will either be smoked like a kipper or come running out. And when it comes out, which it will, we'll be waiting for it, won't we, to blast it to kingdom come.'

Billy heard a match strike and then the twigs begin to crackle. Then he could smell the smoke. The fox wanted to run and began to struggle. But Billy held on tight. He thought of kicking out the back of the cave but knew it was pointless even to begin. There was no time. The game was up and Billy knew it. He was about to call out and surrender when he heard a different voice outside, the quiet voice of an older man that demanded and was used to instant obedience.

'Put that fire out 'fore you set the whole wood alight, you idiots. Stamp it out I tell you, or I'll get ugly. And you wouldn't like me ugly. I don't even like myself when I'm ugly, so just do as you're told and put out that fire!' The voice rose to a sharp command. There was much scuffling outside in the crater. Billy lowered his head to the floor of the cave and could just see their boots stamping out the last of the fire. 'Very well. That will do. Over here the two of you so you can hear me. I'm not going to say this twice. First, you're trespassing on my land. You know who I am and you know you are trespassing. Second, you are poaching. Why else would you have your guns and that little rat of a dog?'

'Only came after a rabbit, didn't we, Jack?'

'That's all, Brigadier, honest.'

'You even lie badly. Is it likely you would go to all that trouble, come all the way up here, to smoke out a rabbit when there's thousands of them hopping about down in the fields? There's more rabbits this year than there's been for years. It's lucky for you I came when I did, 'cos if you'd have caught what you were after then you'd have been up before the Magistrates Monday morning for poaching. Now this time, and only this time, I'll overlook the trespasssing; but if I find you in my woods again I'll get ugly, ugly as sin. Now take that horrible little dog and get yourselves out of here before I change my mind. And one more thing before you go; there's been a swan flying around here the last day or so — seen it myself. Easy things to shoot, swans. If you take a potshot at her, I'll know who it is, remember? If you see it you leave it alone, understand? They're protected, a protected species swans are; but you're not, so get going before my trigger finger gets twitchy.'

Billy's hunched shoulders relaxed as he heard the hunters running off down the hill, the terrier yapping as they went. But he could see one pair of boots were still in the crater and a stick walking with them, as they were coming towards the hole. There was a sound of sniffing and the light was blocked out by a face peering in at them. 'Can't see you,' said the face, that sported a neat white moustache, 'but I know you're in there. Smell a fox a mile away, I can. 'Spect you're out of that earth over in Innocents Copse — saw you when you were little, six of you there were, weren't there? Dashed lucky for you I came by. Only came this way to find that swan. Saw it come down in the woods this morning — funny place for a swan to come down, I thought. Then I spotted the smoke. Came just in time, didn't I? Come September you'll make fine sport for the hounds. So I'll be seeing you again, my fine foxy friend. I'll be the one on the chestnut mare leading the hunt. First over every fence I am: the Master they call me. Be all in pink so you can't miss me. We'll meet again, you can be sure of that. And don't go getting yourself shot in the meantime, will you? Always a pity to waste a good fox.'

The tail of a fox will show no matter how hard he tries to hide it.
Hungarian Proverb

Reynard the Minstrel

from *Le Roman de Renard*

The medieval saga Le Roman de Renard *which collects many of the folk tales and traditions about foxes going back to Aesop's time, was first written in France, and parts of it became known in England in Chaucer's time. Then the first complete translation was made by William Caxton in 1481, based on a Dutch edition rather than the original French.*

In it, Reynard and the other animals are given human characteristics, and it is really a satire on human affairs. There's the weak and greedy King Lion, Bruin the lumbering Bear, Tibert the timorous Cat, and Isegrim the Wolf — thick as ever. Reynard, who has played tricks on them all, has been declared an outlaw. But in this episode he finds an unusual disguise.

The king had proclaimed that anyone who was able to lay hands on Reynard could put him to death on the spot by hanging or by any other means, without bringing him before a court of law.

But Reynard was unperturbed as he made his way through fields and copses, although as ever he was on his guard.

He came to a market town, where he hoped to find some food

for, as ever, he was very hungry, and he stopped in front of a dyer's shop. The master dyer had just made up some yellow dye in a tub, and had gone out of the room to find a rule to measure the cloth with before soaking it. Reynard looked in through the open window, and seeing nobody in the room, jumped inside.

Great was his surprise to find himself plunged into darkness, for he had jumped straight into the tub of dye which was under the window, and he had to dogpaddle around to avoid drowning.

When the dyer came back into the room, he soon heard the noise Reynard was making in his efforts to get out of the tub. As soon as he saw the fox swimming around in the dye, he grabbed something to knock him on the head.

'Desist, dearest sir, desist,' Reyard cried out. 'I may be only an animal, but I am the same as you by profession, and I am sure I could be useful to you. For instance, I don't expect you know how to mix ash in with the dye, and there are other tricks of the trade I've picked up in Paris. But first help me get out of here.'

So the dyer got hold of Reynard by the paw and pulled him out of the tub. As soon as he was back on the ground, Reynard changed his tune.

'You can manage on your own, my brave fellow, for I don't know the first thing about dyeing. I'm so glad I didn't drown in your tub. I congratulate you on the fastness of your dye — what a brilliant yellow this is! No one will recognize me like this, which suits me fine as people don't seem to like me, I can't think why. Farewell then, I'll be off.'

Reynard went back to the woods, and stopped in a clearing to examine himself all over. He laughed to see himself so well disguised. Then he spotted Isegrim the wolf a little distance away, rooting around for his next meal. Now the sight of him did worry Reynard, for the wolf was of robust physique, with an appetite to match, so he hit upon the idea of disguising his voice as if he were a foreigner.

When Isegrim saw Reynard, he was in fact so frightened that

he very nearly took to his heels. He had never seen such a bright yellow animal, and for safety he crossed himself rapidly several times in succession.

Reynard came up to him and greeted him thus: 'Good day, dear lord! Me jolly not speak your language.'

'God keep you, dear friend! Which part of the country are you from? Are you French, even?'

'Nay, my lord, but from Britain. Me jolly English lord, but me jolly lost my fortune and jolly look for my companion. Jolly looked all over England and all over France. Now me not know where to look next . . .'

'And do you have a profession?'

'Ya, me jolly good juggler. But me jolly robbed and beaten yesterday, and my jolly hurdy-gurdy stolen. If me had a jolly hurdy-gurdy, me play jolly good song and good dance for you.'

'And what is your name?'

'Me jolly called Scapegrace. And you, dear lord?'

'My name is Isegrim. But tell me, my friend, have you not come across a dirty redheaded fellow, a crafty villain who loves only himself and deceives everybody? If I could only lay my hands on him, he wouldn't have long to live.'

Reynard kept his head down while he listened to this. 'Upon my faith, my lord, what is this miserable fellow's jolly name?'

'He is called Reynard, the scoundrel. He spends his time making fools of us all. But tell me, dear friend, are you expert enough a minstrel to appear at court with complete confidence?'

'By all the saints of Jerusalem, you jolly not find a better minstrel anywhere.'

'In this case, come with me. I will present you to the king and queen. And I know a peasant who has a fine hurdy-gurdy, and keeps his neighbours awake all night long with it. You shall have it.'

And so they set off together, both well pleased with themselves, and they went straight to the house of the owner of the hurdy-gurdy. They hid in the garden, and when the peasant had gone to bed Isegrim looked into the room. The hurdy-gurdy was hanging from a nail on the wall; the peasant and his wife were snoring loud. Isegrim didn't, however, notice the large dog lying in the shadow of the bed.

'Brother,' he said to Reynard, 'wait for me here while I go in there.' He jumped in through the window, went straight to the spot where the hurdy-gurdy was hanging, took it down and handed it to Reynard through the window.

But Reynard had been thinking hard how he could turn the tables on Isegrim, and as soon as the hurdy-gurdy was in his hands he moved the catch which was keeping the window open, so that it banged shut.

Isegrim assumed the window had shut itself, but he was now a prisoner and in a panic he jumped up against the pane. The noise woke the peasant who stumbled out of bed shouting 'Wake up! Wake up! Thief!' to his wife and children. As he went to get a candle, Isegrim bit him on the behind. But the noise had also woken up the dog who now threw himself on the wolf.

So, with the peasant still yelling, and the wolf still keeping a grip on his nightshirt, and the dog still keeping a grip on the wolf's hindquarters, the noise roused the neighbours who now marched in through the door armed with axes and clubs.

As soon as Isegrim saw the door open, he tore himself away from the dog, leaving a good piece of fur in his jaws. He fled, pursued by the peasants, shouting.

Of his companion, the bright yellow English lord, there was of course no sign. He was crossing the copse, well pleased with the hurdy-gurdy he had acquired. He started practising and after a fortnight could play it very well.

End of the Hunt

from *Peter's Room*

by Antonia Forest

Foxes often evade the hunt by showing a considerable degree of cunning and intelligence — as does the fox described in this extract from Antonia Forest's fifth novel about the Marlow family. The children are spending the Christmas holiday at their home, Trennels, and on a fine crisp morning in early January go out with the local hunt. Twelve-year-old Nicola, who is riding Buster, has just been thrown and is keeping back from the rest of the hunt. Rowan is her elder sister, Mr Tranter is the farm manager, and Oliver Reynolds a local boy. As for 'Charles James', that's an old country name for a fox.

It was then, as she loosened Buster's girth, that she saw the one member of the hunt she had till this moment forgotten: the fox.

He was curled close against the wall, tidy as a cat, watching her, his wedge-shaped, intelligent mask expressing nothing but disdain for two creatures so plainly less fitted for their job than he was for his. Frozen, Nicola stared back at him. He must be the fox they'd been hunting for his coat and brush were muddy and draggled: so hounds had changed foxes after all. Suddenly she saw what it *meant* when you talked of throwing someone off the scent: and you had to be a fox, a cunning Charles James, to do it successfully.

She walked Buster round in a circle. He seemed sound, which was well, for she'd no notion what she'd have done if he hadn't been. She looked again at the contemptuously watching fox, wishing she could stay and see what he did next. But late on a January afternoon when one wasn't too sure where one was and nothing but one's bump of locality insisted that Trennels lay in *that* direction was no time for nature study. She slipped the reins over Buster's head and began to lead him away and, unhurriedly, the fox got on his legs and came too.

She watched him unbelievingly, but there was no doubt about it. They crossed a couple of fields, the fox trotting quietly along a bare six yards to her right and a pace or two in front. The ground began to dip and, through a hunt gate, they came to a sunken lane; the fox slipped into the overgrown ditch and only the whisper of dry leaves and the movement of grasses marked his passage; but he was still there.

The lane sloped gently up, a pale lath of a road with nothing but sky showing above the rise. Lugging Buster behind her like a garden-roller, she watched for another sight of the fox, speculating in a half-suppressed smoulder of excitement what he thought he was doing. Was he *really* coming home with them? *Would* an animal with that face — that contemptuous, self-sufficient, tameless face — ever give itself up? It wasn't possible . . . it *couldn't* be . . . only it would be such heaven if it was . . . Only what would Rowan and Mr Tranter say to a pet fox on a farm? . . .

At the crest of the rise, instinctively, she glanced back. And then she saw why the fox had taken her for his boon companion. Across the field where Buster had fallen the three white hounds, having hunted their fox independently over two fields foiled by sheep, were now feathering stubbornly, remorselessly along a line that was growing cold. As she watched they came to the place where the fox had sat against the wall, paused momentarily and feathered haltingly on across the field. It came to

Nicola, slowly taking in the situation in the light of things
Oliver Reynolds had said, that far from mistaking her for St
Eustace and St Hubert, Patrons of the Chase, the fox had found
her a convenient substitute for a bullock, a sheep, or a patch
of manure: her scent and Buster's might, he had concluded,
drown his own and confuse the hounds.

'*Strewth*,' she said aloud, her admiration divided about
equally between the fox who had thought of it and the white
hounds who had stayed with the line despite his best efforts.

The top of the hill was also a cross-roads: the lane went on
downhill between hedges to the main road or ran east and west,
unhedged, across the Crowlands. The fox, slipping up out of
the ditch, had turned to the eastward road that presumably led
eventually to Trennels. She went with him.

She felt curiously neutral. If she did not want to see Charles
James, so clever, so resourceful, caught at the last, neither did
she want to see the white hounds, so tenacious, so resolute,
disappointed. As she paused to let Buster drink from a little
stream that crossed the road she looked back and saw the
hounds, diminished by distance and luminous in the growing dusk, strike the line on the road. Buster, raising his head
from the stream, saw them too and nickered. 'You better?'
asked Nicola as he stood watching the hounds, ears cocked.
'Because if so, I'm getting up on you again. That was a jolly
hard fall you gave me, let me tell you, and I've walked quite
far enough.'

He really did seem all right again; anyway, his head no
longer drooped. She tightened the girth and remounted. Far
ahead, the fox toddled along the flinty road; far behind, the
hounds followed: but, as if they now understood this particular
confusion of scents, their pace was quickening. The next time
she turned to look, though her pace and Buster's hadn't altered,
the hounds had closed the gap appreciably. And ahead, the
fox's back was arched, his brush dragging: he was tired, he was
done, he would never make the High Men. Involuntarily, not
at all wanting to be in at the death, Nicola pulled Buster to a

stop. And the hounds ran past as if tied to the line, nothing now between them and their quarry.

But the fox was in sight of home. The moorland on the left, rising and falling, concealing and revealing, suddenly disclosed the High Men, the seven barrows which, so it was said, marked the centre of the moor as it had been before the farms and villages bit into it. The heather gave way to grass and the fox turned from the road. And at last the hounds viewed him.

After that it was anyone's hundred yards. The fox raced and the hounds flew, four shapes flashing up the slope into the shelter of the barrows. Shivering, expectant, Nicola sat waiting, but the silence continued unbroken. In the west, hugely crimson in the fume of the horizon, the sun's rim touched the earth; overhead the sky was clear and pale as if it had been glassed over, and by contrast the moorland, when you looked down again, was like darkness rising from the ground. And presently three pale shapes detached themselves from among the barrows and came trotting across the heather towards her, their eyes like garnets in the dusk.

There was no blood on their coats and she supposed the fox had gone safely to ground. But later she was told that these were Fell hounds with no tradition of breaking up their fox. So after all, she would never know what had happened; which, in a way, was as it should be; it left the mystery where it had begun, between the beasts themselves.

A Little Vixen

from *Ivan: Stories of Old Russia*

by Marcus Crouch

The peasant and his good wife had only one son, and he was no great blessing to them because, though good-hearted, he was so thick in the head that he could never get anything right. 'What are we to do with our Ivan?' said the wife one day, when the lad had done something especially silly. 'The only thing he's good at is eating, and we have barely enough food to keep the two of us alive. Let's get rid of him. It's high time he learnt to make his own way in the world.'

So they gave young Ivan their blessing. With it he also took a half-ruined hut in the forest, a cock and five hens (don't forget the hens — they are important) and a horse. Did I say horse? Well, it was not so much a horse as a wretched old broken-backed nag, good for nothing but chewing hay, and he had few teeth left to help him do that.

Ivan rode to the forest and let out his cock and hens to scratch for whatever food they could find. Ivan went to bed. Next morning he thought that he had better go hunting for his dinner. When he had gone out of sight of the hut someone appeared. This was a little vixen who had watched with interest the arrival of her new neighbour. She went sniffing around and soon picked up the smell of tasty hen. In no time she had tracked down a hen and killed it, and wasn't it good to eat? When Ivan came back in the evening he counted his hens and found one missing. 'Poor creature!' he thought. 'I suppose she must have many enemies in the forest. Perhaps a hawk took her.'

When he went off hunting next day he happened to meet the little vixen.

'Where are you going, Ivan?' she asked.

'I am a-hunting, little vixen.'

'Good luck to you then.' And the vixen ran off. And where do you think she went? Why, straight to Ivan's hut, and there she killed a second hen and ate it. It tasted better than the first.

Ivan came home. Another hen missing! Could it possibly be that pretty little vixen who was to blame? On the third day he shut up the cock and the three remaining hens and barred door and window. Then he went hunting.

Soon he met the little vixen.

'Where are you off to this fine day, Ivan?'

'I'm going hunting little vixen?'

'Good luck to you.'

Off ran the vixen, but Ivan turned back and followed her. He watched as she tried the door and the window and sniffed all around the hut. Then she climbed on to the roof and scrambled down the chimney. Ivan ran inside in time to catch her.

'So this is the thief,' he said. 'Good morning, little vixen. So you were going hunting too, were you? It seems that I have caught you.'

'Don't hurt me, Ivan,' said the little vixen. 'That won't do you any good. Let me live and I can be useful to you. You take care of me, and I will get you a rich wife.'

Ivan sat down to think, and he wasn't very good at that exercise. After a while he said: 'Very well. I'll give you a chance, but if you fail me I'll surely cut off that fine tail of yours.'

'You won't regret this,' said the little vixen. 'Now if I am to

find you a wife I shall have to keep fit and well and have plenty
to eat. For a start let me have another of your hens.'

So Ivan killed his third hen and gave it to her. She ate
greedily, then sat a while washing her face. After some thought
she said: 'I have it. You shall marry the Tsar's daughter. They
tell me she is fairly good-looking, and her father will surely give
her enough money for two.'

'How can a fellow like me marry a princess?'

'Never you mind. That's my worry, not yours.'

The little vixen ran off and made her way to the Tsar's
palace. She went in and bowed before the Tsar. 'Greetings,
Your Greatness.'

'Greetings to you too, little vixen,' said the Tsar. 'What tales
of scandal have you brought me today?'

'No scandal; I am here on a matter of state. I come to make
a marriage. You have the bride. I have the groom, and a rich
and handsome one too. His name is Ivan Getrichquick.'

'Where is he then? Can't he speak for himself?'

'Oh, he is far too busy just now,' said the little vixen. 'He is
king of the animals and he has many subjects to care for.'

'What kind of bridegroom are you offering me? Very well,
tell him to send me forty times forty wolves, and then I will
consider his proposal.'

The little vixen went back to the forest, found an open clearing and began to roll over and over on her back. A big
grey wolf came up and stared at her, and said: 'What's up with
you, neighbour? You look as if you have come from a good
feast.'

'Oh dear!' said the little vixen. 'I do wish I hadn't eaten quite
so much. But the Tsar was so pressing. He wouldn't let me
refuse a single mouthful. I wonder you weren't there too,
brother. All the other animals were invited.'

The wolf said: 'Little vixen, we have always been good
friends. Won't you take me with you to the next feast?'

'I think I might manage that. But the Tsar won't be too
pleased to see just a single wolf there. He likes to do things in

style. Call up your tribe and be there tomorrow with forty times forty wolves, and I'll take you all.'

Sure enough, next day all the wolves were waiting, and the little vixen led them to the palace. 'Great Tsar!' she said. 'My master sends you the small gift you asked; forty times forty grey wolves.'

'This is well done,' said the Tsar. 'Now he can send me an equal number of bears.'

In just the same way the little vixen tricked the bears into coming to the palace, and they, like the wolves, went tamely into captivity.

'You have done very well, little vixen,' said the Tsar. 'But what use are all these wild beasts to me? I can't eat wolves, or train bears to run with my hunting dogs. Next time you must bring me forty times forty sables and ermine. At least they will give my family warm coats for the winter.'

The little vixen went home to Ivan's hut. 'Everything is going well,' she said. 'Now you can kill the fourth hen. I have been working very hard and have a great appetite.'

So the fourth hen was eaten, and then the little vixen went back to the clearing in the forest and began rolling. An ermine came slinking by and said to her: 'Whatever is the matter, little vixen? Anyone might think you had the belly-ache.'

'So would you have if you had eaten such a feast as I have just had at the palace. The Tsar was most generous. He piled the tables high and all the animals gorged themselves.'

'If only I had been there,' said the ermine. 'It's not that I am a greedy eater, but I do enjoy fine company. I have always longed to go to Court. Couldn't you take me there, dear vixen?'

'I am sure the Tsar would not think much of having a single ermine at his feast. He likes big numbers. Now, if you could round up, say, forty times forty of your family and your cousins the sables, then I dare say I could get you into the palace.'

So it was that next day forty times forty little animals, all in the richest of fur coats, presented themselves before the Tsar.

'Here they are, Your Greatness, just as you ordered,' said the little vixen, bowing at the ground.

'That is well done,' said the Tsar. 'Your Master has met all my demands. I accept him as my son-in-law. Tell him to come here himself tomorrow. It is high time he had a look at his bride.'

On the following morning the little vixen came alone to the palace. 'My Master sends his regrets, Your Greatness,' she said. 'He would dearly have liked to come himself, but he is over his ears in work today. It is his day for the Treasury, and he will be hard at work till nightfall counting his gold.'

'I am sorry he has so much to do,' said the Tsar. 'It would not take me all day to count *my* gold. I hope we may enjoy his company tomorrow. My daughter grows impatient.'

Home went the little vixen. Poor Ivan was lying in the hut, starving. Since the vixen had been gobbling his hens he had eaten nothing. There was just one hen and the cock left, but he had been reluctant to kill them, for they were all he had left except the horse, and that was too old to make a meal for even a starving man.

'Get up! Get up!' said the little vixen. 'This is your big day. The Tsar is quite won over and is waiting to greet you as his daughter's groom.'

'Are you crazy?' said Ivan. 'How can I go before the Tsar dressed in these rags?'

'Don't argue. Just saddle your horse and away! Leave all the little details to me. But before we go I'll just have that last hen, and the cock too. You won't be needing them any more.'

Ivan was not at all happy about the way things were going, but by now he was used to doing what the vixen told him. He whistled up his wretched horse, threw an old blanket over its bent back, and scrambled up. They went shambling off towards the palace, while the little vixen ran beside them. They came to a little wooden bridge over a river.

'Get down,' said the little vixen. 'Now push hard on the supports of the bridge.'

Ivan did as he was told. The bridge was old and rotten, and it soon went crashing, splashing into the water.

'Now jump into the river.'

The little vixen then ran to the palace and rushed in, shouting: 'Help! Help! What a disaster!'

'Why, whatever has happened?' said the Tsar.

'My poor master! He was riding to visit you, his horse laden with rich gifts, when one of your bridges broke down under him. He is surely drowned.'

At once the Tsar called his servants and told them to run to the bridge, taking fine clothes with them. When they got there they found Ivan lying on the bank. All his ragged clothes had been washed away in the stream, and of his great treasure there was no sign. They picked him up, pummelled him to shake out all the water, and then dressed him in some of the Tsar's own robes.

Back at the palace the Tsar welcomed him joyfully, and ordered that the wedding should take place at once, before anything else could happen to the bridegroom.

So that was that. Ivan married the princess. He lay about all day, singing to himself, eating all he wanted, adored by his wife and admired by his royal father-in-law.

And what about the little vixen? Well, she enjoyed the life of the Court for a time, spoiled and pampered by everyone, petted by the ladies, fed titbits by the gentlemen. It was very nice, but after all no wild creature wants to be a ladies' pet for ever. It wasn't long before she found herself missing the wild wood and the thrill of catching her own food. So she slipped quietly away one day and went back to her own ways.

Fox Hunt

from *Reynard the Fox*

by John Masefield

The fox was strong, he was full of running,
He could run for an hour and then be cunning,
But the cry behind him made him chill,
They were nearer now and they meant to kill.
They meant to run him until his blood
Clogged on his heart as his brush with mud,
Till his back bent up and his tongue hung flagging,
And his belly and brush were filthed from dragging;
Till he crouched stone-still, dead-beat and dirty,
With nothing but teeth against the thirty.
And all the way to that blinding end
He would meet with men and have none his friend:
Men to holloa and men to run him,
With stones to stagger and yells to stun him,
Men to head him, with whips to be at him,
Teeth to mangle and mouths to eat him.

And all the way, that wild high crying,
To cold his blood with the thought of dying,
The horn and the cheer, and the drum-like thunder
Of the horsehooves stamping the meadows under.
He tipped his brush and went with a will
For the Sarsen Stones on Wan Dyke Hill.

What is a fox hound's favourite food?
Fox tail soup!

Fox Magic

from *The Steps Up the Chimney*

by William Corlett

*Many people feel sympathy for foxes, but it takes a little magic for someone
to actually feel like one, as does William in this extract from the first
part of* The Magicians' House *quartet. William and his sisters are
staying with their uncle Jack in a remote part of Wales over the Christmas
holidays. They quickly become involved in some magical goings-on con-
nected with the old house and the Magician who lived there in Elizabethan
times. It's back to reality and practical problems as the house becomes cut
off by snowdrifts just at the time Jack's girlfriend's baby is due. William
sets off to get help, and encounters Cinnabar the Fox.*

The fox was waiting for him at the side of the road, its long,
sleek body a dazzling red in contrast with the grey and white
of the snow.

William walked towards it, extending his hand, rather as
you would when approaching a dog, in a gesture of friendship.
But the fox was no dog. It watched William with suspicious
eyes and shied away before he got close enough to touch
him.

'Here, boy!' William said, surprised by this reaction, and

trying to make his voice sound enticing. He crouched in the snow, his hand still extended towards the fox, trying to coax it towards him. But the fox only slunk further away from him and then turned and scampered round behind a mound of snow that covered a low stone wall. There it paused and William could see it skulking at a distance, watching him still.

'What's the matter?' William called out. 'I thought you were my friend.'

But the fox only stared, body tense, ready to run if William made a move towards it.

'Oh, come on!' William shouted, crossly. Then, when he still got no reaction, he turned his back on the fox and looked instead at the long line of tree-covered hills where Jack was lying waiting for him.

The footprints of the fox were still just visible in a vague line, leading across the snow covered field to a distant grey stone wall.

William remembered the sensation of flying as they leapt that wall. Then he frowned and shook his head. How could he have? The fox could have leapt the wall. But not him. And where were his footprints? True it was still snowing quite hard and they could have been covered by now but, in that case, why weren't the prints of the fox covered also?

'You really don't know, do you?' a voice in his head said.

'Know what?' William asked, aloud.

'How you got here,' the voice whispered.

'Of course I do,' William replied, feeling hot.

'Talking to yourself?' the voice in his head whispered.

William looked around, uncomfortably, hoping that no one had been listening to him. Talking to oneself was, after all, the first sign of madness.

The fox was sitting in the snow, at the side of the wall, watching him. William thought it had a rather sly expression.

'What are you waiting for, anyway?' William shouted at it.

The fox stood up on its four legs, its tail held aloft like a burning flame, and stared at him impassively.

'Well?' William demanded, feeling uncomfortable. The fox had a superior air that was most unnerving.

'Go on,' William shouted again, waving his arm. 'Go away. I thought you'd help me. Well, if you won't, just go away.'

The fox yawned, and stretched its body. The breath from its mouth smoked on the frosty air. Then it lifted its head, listening.

'Please,' William called, in a contrite voice, 'I really do need your help.'

Slowly the fox turned and looked at him. They stood staring at each other, surrounded by the vast expanse of gleaming white. The clouds were higher now and the falling snow was turning from big cotton wool blobs to a fine powder. The wind had dropped and a profound silence had settled over the countryside; that silence that only the snow brings, the sort of silence that you think you can touch, the sort of silence that clings to you and covers you and wraps itself around you.

Once again, as had happened several times recently, William felt peculiarly displaced. Perhaps it was the thick layer of snow that gave the country such a strangely anonymous blankness. Perhaps it was the extreme exertion that he had just been through that made William dizzy. Or perhaps . . .

'Perhaps it's the Magician's magic,' the fox whispered.

'You feel it too?' William asked.

'Always,' the fox replied. 'But I belong to the Magician, and not to you, little boy. I'm a wild creature. No use trying to train me like a farm dog. Understand? I hunt to survive. There's nothing soft in my life. My vixen and her cubs need me to be strong and sharp. Let me tell you, little boy, if you travel with me, it will be danger all the way.' The fox stretched again and licked its flank in a nonchalant way. Then it stared back at William with piercing eyes. 'There's a hunt round here,' it whispered.

The words made William tremble and look over his shoulder. He could feel the hair on the back of his neck stirring.

'Now?' he asked, in his head. 'Is the hunt out now?'

'No, not now,' the voice in his head continued. 'The weather's too harsh for the humans. But we have to be careful. Come on, I'm hungry. There are some hens along the way.'

As the voice spoke, William sprang forward and a moment later he could feel his paws lightly skimming across the surface of the snow.

'But what about Uncle Jack?' he thought.

'Can't do anything till we've eaten,' the fox told him.

William could hear the hens before he saw them. They were in a wooden house, with a wire mesh cage in front of it. There was a gap in the wire.

'No!' William cried out, just in time. And he did so with such force that the fox sprang away from him, surprised, and somehow the two bodies became separate again.

'I couldn't eat a raw chicken,' William explained.

The fox sighed and stared at him pityingly.

'Humans!' it said in a withering voice. 'Call yourselves animals? You're neither one thing nor the other,' and without another word it squeezed under the wire and prowled towards the door of the hen house.

William backed away. He wasn't squeamish about the sight of blood. But the thought of what now was going to happen appalled him. He didn't mind hitching the odd lift with the fox, but he refused to guzzle a raw chicken with him. He couldn't do that for anyone. Not even a Magician.

A Battle

from *Fox's Feud*

by Colin Dann

At the start of Colin Dann's Farthing Wood *animal saga, Fox and a
group of animals — including Kestrel and Whistler the Heron — move
from their old home threatened by redevelopment to settle in the White Deer
nature reserve where they will be protected. But their arrival is resented
by some of the previous inhabitants — partly because there is a shortage
of food — and among them is Scarface, the old battle-scarred fox. When
he kills one of Fox's cubs, Fox decides he must act.*

*Bold is another of Fox's cubs, and he features in a later story in the
saga, and in the extract* The Urban Fox *(page 74). Ranger is one of
Scarface's cubs.*

There was an excited buzz of conversation in the set as Fox
crept into the tunnel and vigorously shook himself in prepar-
ation. Vixen followed him worriedly.

'Must you do this, dearest?' she asked him.

'It's our only hope,' answered her mate. 'If we stay here we
shall all be slaughtered or starved to death.'

'But Scarface is treachery itself,' Vixen urged. 'You can't trust him. Even if he should accept your challenge, he might set the others on you if you showed signs of winning.'

Fox smiled gently at her. 'I know you are concerned for me and, were it just you and me, things might be different. But I must take this risk for the others' sake.'

'Oh, why must they always depend on *you* ?' she whispered fiercely. But she knew Fox would not be budged.

He answered: 'It was my quarrel in the first place. I'm doing no more than my duty.'

Then she watched him go out into the sunlight.

At Fox's appearance Scarface yapped in triumph. But there was no movement towards him as yet. Only Tawny Owl and Whistler flew to a closer perch, while Kestrel hovered low in the air, ready to swoop down if necessary.

Fox looked at Scarface steadily and then his glance turned to the other assembled throng, who were fidgeting nervously. He noticed Ranger had placed himself well back in the rear.

'You have come in strength, I see,' said Fox coolly. 'Do you need all these to overcome me?'

'You have your followers, also,' Scarface growled.

'No.' Fox shook his head. 'No followers — only friends.'

'Oh yes — your precious friends. Well, today they are going to regret they were ever your friends.'

'You have no dispute with them,' Fox said. 'It is me you fear.'

Scarface's eyes blazed. 'Fear?' he barked. 'You talk to me of fear? I didn't acquire these scars by being afraid. I fear nothing!'

'An idle boast,' Fox answered provokingly. 'I say you fear me; and I believe your fear has governed all your actions since I first came to the Park.'

Scarface tensed himself and seemed about to spring on the taunting Fox, who watched him through narrowing eyes. But then his body relaxed again. 'You are clever,' he said. 'I see what game you're playing.'

'Game?' Fox queried. 'I haven't come to play, but to fight.'

The tribe of foxes began to mill about, murmuring to each other. It was clear their confidence did not match their leader's.

'You are an arrogant creature.' Scarface replied with a cynical grin. 'You would set yourself against the whole pack?'

'Not I,' said Fox. 'Why would I wish to fight them? Only *you* have made yourself my enemy.'

'Oh, so you wish to fight *me*?' Scarface chuckled.

'To settle this issue once and for all — yes.'

'You're a cool customer, I'll give you that. But, you see, the odds are against you.'

'I believe we have an even chance,' Fox replied, 'in a fair fight.'

Scarface fell silent. He seemed to have fallen into a trap. If he should refuse the fight, he would be taken for a coward. He looked up with a grim smile. 'Why do you offer yourself as a sacrifice?' he asked with a grudging respect.

'Because I fight on one condition,' answered Fox. 'If I prove victorious, my friends are to go unharmed.'

Scarface broke into a harsh laugh. 'And all this for a collection of mice and hedgehogs,' he rasped. His face became as hard as stone. 'All right, you have your wish,' he growled. 'And when I've killed you, I'll fight your cubs, one by one, and destroy them all.'

Fox was quite aware of the seriousness of his situation. He had laid his challenge at the feet of an animal more hardened and experienced in battle than any in the whole Reserve. The only advantage on his side was his comparative youth, for he had no illusions about the other's strength and cunning.

The two animals faced each other as if assessing the opponent's qualities. Fox decided to take a defensive stance and so, at Scarface's first rush, he had ample time to swing aside. Then Scarface again rushed headlong at him but Fox dropped flat on his belly, and Scarface's jaws snapped at the air. But the old warrior turned quickly and bit savagely at Fox's scruff. Fox broke free, leaving Scarface with a good mouthful of his fur. The other foxes watched in silence as their leader paused before his next move, while his adversary backed steadily away.

Scarface raced forward again and, with a leap, crashed right
on top of Fox, bowling him over and driving all the breath from
his body. As Fox lay, gasping painfully, Scarface barked in
triumph and, teeth bared, lunged for his throat. But Fox
scrambled clear in the nick of time and stood with heaving
sides, his lungs labouring with difficulty. From the corner of his
eye, he saw the heads of Vixen, Badger and Bold at the
entrance to the set, watching in dismay. With a supreme effort
he gulped down more air and held himself ready again. Now
Scarface came in close, snapping left and right with his awful
jaws, while Fox stepped further and further back at his
advance. He felt his enemy's teeth and knew that Scarface had
tasted blood. They reached a patch of uneven ground and Fox
stumbled, his back legs stepping into a dip of the land. Scarface
got a grip on his muzzle and held on, biting deep. But Fox
kicked out fiercely with his front legs, knocking him back on
to his haunches, and then followed up with a lightning thrust
at his front legs.

Scarface yelped with pain as Fox's teeth sank into his lower
leg and he tried desperately to shake him off. But Fox held fast,
pinioning him to the ground and, as Scarface fell on his back
trying to wrestle free, Fox transferred his grip to the other
animal's throat. To kill was not in Fox's mind but he resolved
to weaken Scarface so much so that he would be in no mood
for fighting for long days to come. Even as Scarface struggled
at his mercy, Kestrel zoomed down with a message: 'The
Warden is coming this way.'

Fox maintained his advantage for a few moments longer and
then loosened his grip. Scarface lay still, his breath whistling
agonizingly through his open jaws. Fox saw the approaching
human figure and then ran for Badger's set. Ranger and the rest
of the band had already dispersed. The Warden came up to the
injured Scarface and bent to help him. As he did so, the animal
made a feeble snap at his extended hand, rolled over on to his
feet and limped away, his brush hanging in a dejected manner
between his legs.

In the set Fox was greeted as a hero again. Most of the animals thought Scarface was dead.

'I didn't kill him,' Fox said as he sat heavily down by Badger while Vixen carefully and soothingly licked his wounds.

'Why not? Why not?' cried Vole. 'Let us finish him off now!'

'The Warden came,' Vixen explained quietly, pausing for a moment in her work. 'But Scarface is defeated. He won't be back.'

An old fox is not easily snared.
Proverb

The Fox and the Vet

from *Free Spirit*

by Michael Chambers·

Michael Chambers, growing up in no wilder a place than the Midlands, had considerable success in taming the vixen Ferdi. She became great friends with his gentle labrador Sniff and the Alsatian Big, and there were hilarious games between them.

Although Ferdi was almost house-trained, she kept her foxy ways, and had such endearing habits as hiding chocolate biscuits under the carpet as a store.

When there was a fear she had caught distemper — a disease which affects dogs and foxes — his father had to call in a vet.

The vet had come from the same practice that I had used on several occasions and I knew him fairly well. He was the youngest of three who shared the practice. There had been no problems with Sniff, of placid nature and even more so now, being lowered by the effects of the disease. He finished with her very quickly. My folks then told him about Ferdi.

Yes, he'd confirmed, foxes were susceptible to distemper. 'She had also better have a shot.'

This time he was about to earn his fee.

It's hard to imagine a greater contrast in two animals of similar size than between a naturally friendly, cooperative and sick dog, and a badly scared, highly suspicious, extremely fit fox.

The cage was about three feet six inches high. Ferdi predictably backed off as far from the door as possible, so there was no difficulty in getting into the cage. My father closed the door after him. Now began what Dad described as the most one-sided contest since the All Blacks played the Women's Institute. Forced to sit on his heels and shuffle about like a clockwork toy, the vet tried to crowd her into a corner; charged hypodermic clutched in one hand, he tried to drive her back with the other. Even in the close confines of the cage she evaded him with ease, adding to his discomfort by giving off her pungent defensive scent.

Dad described an amusing scene. No matter what the vet did, Ferdi always seemed to be standing behind him so that he was forever waddling round to try to face her while she merely slipped round behind him again. The top of his head already sore from scraping the wire roof, his crouching posture eventually induced an attack of cramp in his thigh. With a yell he rolled on to his back and lay flat across the floor of the cage, bracing his leg out straight to pull the painful knots out of his muscles. Ferdi, made even more fearful by his yells, added insult to injury by jumping over his supine body. Gradually the cramp spasm released its grip and he sat up.

Since he was already rolling around the floor, which was also wire netting, with the grass of the lawn poking through it, and realized that in this position he could easily span the entire width of the cage, he began to edge his way towards Ferdi, by now every inch the hunted wild animal. Several times she jumped over him; each time he had to work his way back in the opposite direction. Eventually he managed to grab her brush as she attempted to pass him yet again. She promptly returned the compliment by grabbing his thumb and he let her go again.

That was enough. Round one was over; he crawled to the door and Dad let him out. There was no doubt that the fox was a long way ahead on points. He cleaned up his thumb, applied a plaster, had a cup of tea (what else in a crisis?) and they considered tactics very carefully.

Dad went to the garage and produced an old door almost exactly the right size, if placed sideways, to block off the full width of the cage.

To Mr Harrison the whole thing had now become a matter of professional pride. With a plea to my parents, 'Please don't ever tell my boss I wore gloves,' he donned a heavy leather gauntlet, a relic of my own or my brother's motor cycling days.

Fortunately, the door to the cage was right in one corner and so the other door could be slid across one end of the cage without trouble. It was difficult to manoeuvre, but advancing very slowly behind this barrier he forced Ferdi back until her only refuge was the sleeping box; into this she retreated. The fox was now trapped, with the door against the small entrance to the box, but Mr Harrison was on the other side of the door. He moved back, let the door fall towards him and scrambled over it to the box as fast as he could go. Luckily Ferdi made no attempt to leave the box.

Then he readied his hypodermic, thrust the gauntleted hand into the box, grabbed a hind leg and pulled enough out to present her rump as a target for the needle. It only remained to extract vet and door from the cage and the operation was over.

Round two pretty convincingly to the vet, and an honourable draw declared.

Fight with an Eagle

from *Red Fox*

by Charles G. D. Roberts

Considered to be among the finest animal stories ever written, this story,
first published in 1905, is set in the forests of eastern Canada, the Ringwaak.
It relates Red Fox's battle for survival against the elements — sub-zero
temperatures in winter, a drought and forest fire in summer — and his
encounters with other wild animals such as bears, minks and porcupines.
He also has some near misses with the local woodsman Jabe Smith's 'spitting
devil' (gun), but here his battle for supremacy is with a white-headed eagle.

Red Fox and his family had few neighbours to intrude upon his
privacy. Over the naked ridge-crest the winds blew steadily,
sometimes humming to a gale; but they never disturbed the quiet
of that deep pocket in the rocks, with its little plot of bright, bare
soil where the young foxes played and sunned themselves. No
matter what the direction of the wind, no matter from what quarter
the driven rain came slanting, the hollow was perfectly protected.
On the top of the bare rock which partly overhung it from the north,
Red Fox would sometimes lie and watch, with eyes half-closed
and mouth half-open, the world of green and brown and purple
and blue outspread below and around him. Far down, on both

sides of the ridge, he would note the farmers of both valleys getting
in their crops, and the ceaseless, monotonous toiling of the patient
teams. And far over to the eastward he would eye the bold heights
of old Ringwaak, with the crow-haunted fir-groves on its flanks,
and plan to go foraging over there some day, for sheer restlessness
of curiosity.

But though neighbours were few up here, there was one pair
on whom Red Fox and his mate looked with strong disapproval,
not unmixed with anxiety. On an inaccessible ledge, in a ravine
a little way down the other side of the ridge, towards Ringwaak,
was the nest of a white-headed eagle. It was a great, untidy,
shapeless mass, a cart-load of sticks, as it were, apparently dropped
from the skies upon this bare ledge, but in reality so interwoven
with each point of rock, and so braced in the crevices, that no
tempest could avail to jar its strong foundations. In a hollow in
the top of this mass, on a few wisps of dry grass mixed with feathers
and fur, huddled two half-naked, fierce-eyed nestlings, their
awkward, sprawling, reddish bodies beginning to be sprinkled
with short black pin-feathers. All around the outer edges of this
huge nest and on the rocks below it, were the bones of rabbits and
young lambs and minks, and woodchucks, with claws and little
hoofs, and bills, and feathers; a hideous conglomeration that
attested both the appetites of the nestlings and the hunting prowess
of the wide-winged, savage-eyed parents.

Of the eagle pair, the larger, who was the female, had her aerial
range over Ringwaak, and the chain of lonely lakes the other side
of Ringwaak. But the male did all his hunting over the region of
the settlements and on towards the Ottanoonsis Valley. Every
morning, just after sunrise, his great wings went winnowing
mightily just over the crest of the ridge, just over the lofty hollow
where Red Fox had his lair. And as the dread shadow, with its
sinister rustling of stiff pinions, passed by, the little foxes would
shrink back into their den, well taught by their father and mother.

When the weather was fine and dry, it was Red Fox's custom
to betake himself, on his return from the night's hunting, to his
safe 'lookout' on the rocky summit above the den, and there, resting

with his nose on his fore paws, to watch the vast and austere dawn roll up upon the world. Sometimes he brought his prey — when it was something worthwhile, like a weasel or woodchuck or duck or rabbit — up to his lonely place to be devoured at leisure, beyond the solicitude of his mate and the irrepressible whimperings of the puppies. He would lie there in the mystic spreading of the grey transparencies of dawn till the first long fingers of gold light touched his face, and the thin flood of amber and rose washed all over the bald top of the rock. He would watch, with ceaseless interest, the mother eagle swoop down with narrowed wings into the misty shadows of the valley, then mount slowly, questing, along the slopes of Ringwaak, and finally soar high above the peak, a slowly gyrating speck against the young blue. He would watch the male spring into the air resolutely, beat up the near steep, wing low over his rock, and sail majestically down over the valley farms. Later he would see them return to the nest, from any point of the compass as it might chance, sometimes with a big lake trout snatched from the industrious fish-hawks, sometimes with a luckless mallard from the reed-beds southward, sometimes with a long-legged, pathetic white lamb from the rough upland pastures. With keenest interest, and no small appreciation, he would watch the great birds balance themselves, wings half-uplifted, on the edge of the nest, and with terrible beak and claws rend the victim to bloody fragments. He marvelled at the insatiable appetites of those two ugly nestlings, and congratulated himself that his four playful whelps were more comely and less greedy.

One morning when, in the grey of earliest dawn, he climbed to his retreat with a plump woodchuck in his jaws, it chanced it was in no hurry for his meal. Dropping the limp body till he should feel more relish for it, he lay down to rest and contemplate the waking earth. As he lay, the sun rose. The female eagle sailed away towards Ringwaak. The male beat up, and up, high above the ridge, and Red Fox paid no more attention to him, being engrossed in the antics of a porcupine which was swinging in a tree-top far below.

Suddenly he heard a sharp, hissing rush of great wings in the air just above him, and glanced upward astonished. The next instant he felt a buffeting wind, huge wings almost smote him in the face — and the dead woodchuck, not three feet away, was snatched up in clutching talons, and borne off into the air. With a furious snarl he jumped to his feet; but the eagle, with the prize dangling from his claws, was already far out of reach, slanting down majestically towards his nest.

The insolence and daring of this robbery fixed in Red Fox's heart a fierce desire for vengeance. He stole down to the ravine that held the eyrie, and prowled about for hours, seeking a place where he could climb to the ledge. It was quite inaccessible, however; and the eagles, knowing this, looked down upon the prowlings with disdainful serenity. Then he mounted the nearby cliff and peered down directly into the nest. But finding himself still as far off as ever, and the eagles still undisturbed, he gave up the hope of an immediate settlement of his grudge and lay in wait for the chances of the wilderness. He was frank enough, however, in his declaration of war; for whenever the eagle went winging low over his rocky lookout, he would rise and snarl up at him defiantly. The great bird would bend his flight lower, as if to accept this challenge; but having a wise respect for those long jaws and white fangs which the fox displayed so liberally, he took care not to come within their reach.

A few days later, while Red Fox was away hunting down in the valley, the fox-puppies were playing just in the mouth of the den when they saw their slim mother among the rocks. In a puppy-like frolic of welcome they rushed to meet her, feeling secure in her nearness. When they were half-way across the open in front of the den, there came a sudden shadow above them. Like a flash they scattered — all but one, who crouched flat and stared irresolutely. There was a dreadful whistling sound in the air, a pounce of great, flapping wings and wide-reaching talons, a strangled yelp of terror. And before the mother fox's leap could reach the spot, the red puppy was snatched up and carried away to the beaks of the eaglets.

When he learned about this, Red Fox felt such fury as his

philosophic spirit had never known before. He paid another futile visit to the foot of the eagles' rock; and afterwards, for days, wasted much time from his hunting in the effort to devise some means of getting at his foe. He followed the eagle's flight and foraging persistently, seeking to be on the spot when the robber made a kill. But the great bird had such a wide range that this effort seemed likely to be a vain one. In whatever region Red Fox lay in wait, in some other would the eagle make his kill. With its immeasurable superiority in power of sight, the royal marauder had no trouble in avoiding his enemy's path, so that Red Fox was under surveillance when he least suspected it.

It was one day when he was not thinking of eagles or of vengeance that Red Fox's opportunity came. It was towards evening, and for a good half-hour he had been quite out of sight, watching for a wary old woodchuck to venture from its hole. As he lay there, patient and moveless, he caught sight of a huge black snake gliding slowly across the open glade. He hesitated, in doubt whether to attack the snake or keep on waiting for the woodchuck. Just then came that whistling sound in the air which he knew so well. The snake heard it too, and darted towards the nearest tree, which chanced to be a bare young birch sapling. It had barely reached the foot of the tree when the feathered thunderbolt out of the sky fell upon it, clutching it securely with both talons about a foot behind the head.

Easily and effectively had the eagle made his capture; but, when he tried to rise with his prey, his broad wings beat the air in vain. At the instant of attack the snake had whipped a couple of coils of its tail around the young birch-tree, and that desperate grip the eagle could not break. Savagely he picked at the coils, and then at the reptile's head, preparing to take the prize off in sections if necessary.

Red Fox's moment, long looked for and planned for, had come. His rush from cover was straight and low, and swift as a dart; and his jaws caught the eagle a slashing cut on the upper leg. Fox-like, he bit and let go; and the great bird, with a yelp of pain and amazement, whirled about, striking at him furiously with beak

and wings. He got one buffet from those wings which knocked
him over; and the eagle, willing to shirk the conflict, disengaged
his talons from the snake and tried to rise. But in an instant Red
Fox was upon him again, reaching up for his neck with a lightning-
like ferocity that disconcerted the bird's defence. At such close
quarters the bird's wings were ineffective, but his rending beak
and steel-like talons found their mark in Red Fox's ruddy coat,
which was dyed with crimson in a second.

For most foxes the king of the air would have proved more than
a match; but the strength and cleverness of Red Fox put the chance
of battle heavily in his favour. In a few seconds he would have
had the eagle overborne and helpless, and would have reached
his throat in spite of beak and claw. But at this critical moment
the bird found an unexpected and undeserved ally. The snake
which he had attacked, being desperately wounded, was thrashing
about in the effort to get away to some hiding. Red Fox happened
to step upon it in the struggle; and instantly, though blindly, it
threw a convulsive coil about his hind legs. Angrily he turned,
and bit at the constricting coil. And while he was tearing at it,
seeking to free himself, the eagle recovered, raised himself with
difficulty, and succeeded in flopping up into the air. Bedraggled,
bloody, and abjectly humiliated, he went beating over the forest
towards home; and Red Fox, fairly well satisfied in spite of the
incompleteness of his victory, proceeded to refresh himself by a
hearty meal of snake. He felt reasonably certain that the big eagle
would give both himself and his family a wide berth in the future.

The Fox Who Came to Town

by Stanley Cook

When the fox decided to move
He was far too knowing and clever
To travel by a busy road
And risk being hit or run over.

He went along the railway line
Where trains once ran to town,
Where the track was taken up
And the signals taken down.

He passed the empty stations:
No passengers were waiting there,
The booking halls were closed
And no one asked for his fare.

He reached the middle of town,
With its noisy, busy streets,
And quietly stole about,
Looking for something to eat.

The Urban Fox

from *The Fox Cub Bold*

by Colin Dann

Young Bold was first encountered in an earlier extract from Colin Dann's Farthing Wood *series; the biggest and, well,* boldest *cub of Fox's litter, he wanted to prove his independence by leaving the White Deer nature reserve and fend for himself. But times are hard, particularly after he has been wounded in the leg, and with winter coming he decides to try his luck in a town. Among the friends he has made along the way is Robber the crow, and they have agreed to pool their food resources.*

When night fell, it was Bold's turn to make a foray. Robber had gone to roost in a secluded place at the top of a tall tree, leaving the young fox to gather his courage together. For a long time the noise from the town continued unabated. But as the nocturnal hours marched by, a comparative peace descended, only occasionally interrupted by a sudden, strident sound. Then Bold was ready to move.

He went limping across the fields, now bathed by a fitful moonlight, and made for the black shapes of the humans' dwellings. He paused often to test the air as he went. His powerful sense of smell detected a host of strange scents, none of which

was familiar to him. But he pressed on, prepared to take cover
only if the smell of dog or that of Man himself was recognizable.
The first group of buildings he came to lay in complete
darkness. Walls or fences bounded them and their plots of land,
and Bold skulked along these barriers like a shadow, searching
for an opening. For, unlike other animals of his kind, he could
not jump. He soon realized he was indeed handicapped for he
was thus effectively debarred from entering most of the
gardens. Of course he was able to contort himself wonderfully
to slink through the slightest gap; he could flatten himself to
scramble underneath an obstacle; he could even dig; but any
sort of leap was absolutely beyond his scope.

On that first exploratory roam around Bold succeeded in
visiting a number of yards and gardens and this was when he
discovered what was to be the mainstay of his food supply for
weeks to come — the dustbin. Once he had got used to the clang
that some of them made what a remarkable collection of
unwanted scraps he found in these receptacles! There was
always something, it seemed, of which use could be made. It
was almost as if the improvident humans had attempted to
encourage him to feast upon these puzzling little dumps of food.
Bold accepted each and every thing gratefully as he came to
realize that his survival appeared to be ensured. Winter would
not claim him as a victim after all.

His inquisitiveness kept him so busy that he forgot how far
he was from his new hideaway. Dawn was stealing across the
sky as he hastily set off on the return journey. He did not
remember his duty to Robber, for he went empty-jawed. Back
along the human paths he hobbled until he reached the playing
fields. The noise had started up again as he made haste across
the wide open space. Only when he reached the waste plot did
he realize he had not kept his bargain.

Robber arrived at the spot, intending to leave Bold to snooze
peacefully. He waddled along the ground, jerkily turning his
head this way and that as he searched for the delicacy he was
sure the fox would have brought him. Of course, there was

none. Robber wondered if Bold had not returned. He flew up
to a branch and spied out the land. No sign of any animal.
Then he 'cawed' three or four times loudly and harshly with
annoyance.

'I'm here,' Bold owned up.

'Ah, now I see you,' said the crow. 'Were you unsuccessful?'

'Er — no, not exactly,' Bold replied awkwardly.

There was a pause. 'Oh! So our bargain is to be a one-sided
sort, is it?' remarked the crow.

'Not at all,' Bold hastened to explain. 'I — I was caught rather
far from home when dawn broke.'

'I see. Well, as you are still in my debt I shall not be expected
to find *you* anything now?'

'Of course not,' said Bold in a small voice.

Robber flew away immediately, without another word. Bold
did feel a little shamed and decided he would make up for his
failure on his next trip.

The next evening came round wonderfully quickly.
December arrived with a stinging squall of sleet that drove
across the open fields in a spray of ice-needles. The fox's eyes
smarted as he battled against the blast, cursing the handicap of
his limp. But there was shelter amongst Man's buildings and
Bold again began to enjoy his exploring. In one yard he found
two bowls, one containing milk; the other fish. He greatly
appreciated the thoughtfulness of the humans who had supplied
them. There didn't seem to be any other animals nearby to
claim the bowls' contents.

He went on cautiously, snapping up pieces of bread missed
by birds in one garden, knocking over bins in another to raid
the pungent-smelling collections that spilled from them. He had
learnt to retire quickly behind a plant or other screen as the bin
crashed down; then, if nothing happened after a few minutes,
he slunk back to select his pickings. Sometimes the clattering
he caused did bring a human into the open. On those occasions,
Bold was out of the garden and well away from the scene before
he could be noticed.

On this evening he was to find that there were competitors
for his food. He was looking into a large fenced area of lawn
and flower beds behind an imposing house. The sleet fell slant-
wise across the grass in a sort of mist. Out of the shadows
around the building there trotted a brisk, confident-looking fox
that seemed to know exactly what it was about. Bold's muscles
tautened as he watched. The animal stepped lightly across the
grass with a fluid grace that was a perfect illustration of health
and vitality. It made straight for a stone bird-table, the flat top
of which was nearly two metres from the ground. With the most
enviable agility the fox leapt in one flowing movement up to the
top. There it stood, fearlessly surveying its surroundings,
before snatching up the remnants of the birds' leavings. Bold
was entranced. He knew it to be a female, and he was as full
of admiration for her strength as for her grace and elegance.
He thought of his own poor frame; his hobbling walk; his
inability to jump, and he shrank back timidly to avoid being
detected.

As luck would have it, after making a brief circuit of the
garden, the vixen came straight towards Bold. Instinctively he
flattened himself against the ground. She leapt the fence
effortlessly and landed about three metres from him. Some
slight involuntary movement on Bold's part betrayed his
presence. She turned and looked at him calmly. No trace of
surprise or curiosity was shown by her. For a few moments they
stared into each others' eyes, then she swung round and trotted
coolly away as if he had been of no more interest than a piece
of wood.

Bold felt humiliated by her disregard. Although there was no
reason for her to pay him any attention, her nonchalance only
made him all the more conscious of his poor appearance. He
felt that her reaction might have been quite different had she
seen him as he had once been in those first glorious weeks after
he had left the Nature Reserve. Now he was indeed quite
another animal. His physical deficiencies assumed a new pro-
portion in his mind and his confidence fell to a low ebb. What

a cringing, struggling scrap of a creature he had become! He
crawled away from the fence, his brush hanging lifelessly
between his legs. Why continue the fight? He would be better
off out of it all.

But life had to go on and Bold had to go on. He pulled a
meaty-looking bone from the next container he upset and
began his slow, sad, homeward journey. At least Robber would
have no cause for complaint this time.

Four Little Foxes

by Lew Sarett

Speak gently, Spring, and make no sudden sound;
For in my windy valley, yesterday, I found
New-born foxes squirming on the ground—
        Speak gently.

Walk softly, March, forbear the bitter blow;
Her feet within a trap, her blood upon the snow,
The four little foxes saw their mother go—
        Walk softly.

Go lightly, Spring, oh, give them no alarm;
When I covered them with boughs to shelter them from harm,
The thin blue foxes suckled at my arm—
        Go lightly.

Step softly, March, with your rampant hurricane;
Nuzzling one another, and whimpering with pain,
The new little foxes are shivering in the rain—
        Step softly.

The Trapped Vixen

from *Out of the Wild*

by Mike Tomkies

Foxes are wild animals, distrustful (for good reason) of humans, and do not make good pets. But a few people have, with considerable patience, been successful in training foxes to some degree, wanting to study them at close quarters for a while before releasing them back into the wild.

Mike Tomkies, who lives in a remote part of Scotland, has taken in a number of wild animals — often injured in traps — over the years. Moobli is his large Alsatian, a gentle giant who often makes friends with the animals — when allowed to. The vixen Aspen has other ideas, however.

'Her name is Aspen, and she is very shy,' David told me.

It was true. While the larger vixen, about a month older and paler in colour, frisked about and watched us with bright orange eyes, Aspen crept timidly, furtively, into a hiding place between two logs.

David took hold of her thick brush and rear legs, gently hauled her out and handed her to me. As I put my left hand under her chest and my right hand over her shoulders, I could feel her heart thudding with fear. She struggled a little but made no attempt to bite. She was a lovely chubby little creature with thick lustrous dark-auburn fur, and she had a big white tip on her tail. Across the top of her right front paw was a livid white scar where the trap had got her. It had healed now and all the claws were there. We put her carefully into the den box with some food, then set the box on the front seat of my truck. Her eyes, brown at this stage, switched about watching all my movements, showing whites at their edges. When Moobli put his head over the seat to sniff close, she snapped at him and he withdrew quickly. When I put my hand near, for her to sniff, she snapped at that too. She would not be easy to tame.

We camped out overnight, for just a few hours' sleep, then boated her home. Quickly I made a makeshift pen in a corner of the kitchen and put her in it. All my movements had to be slow or she spat like a cat and dashed about. When I put the den box in she darted inside and stayed there.

Next morning I was worried because she had not touched any of the meats or milk. It took nearly an hour to slide one hand behind her and coax and ease her out. Once she made a symbolic bite at my fingers but I felt no teeth, just a soft snap as from a duck's beak. I lifted her out, set her on my lap and spent a long time talking soothingly to her, telling her she was safe, constantly stroking her fur. I noticed that her thick black whiskers were longer than any cat's. Gently I examined her injured paw. It was swollen into a club shape and some of the toe bones had congealed rather than healed properly, for they did not have the same capability of movement as those in the other front foot. As her elfin face, topped by its two huge stiff ears, stared into mine I thought that if those who put down snares and traps could see her at that moment they might have second thoughts.

I held milk out to her in a green saucer. She sniffed, black pointed nose trembling, then to my delight began to lap it up, until she had drunk a quarter of a lamb's bottleful. I put her back in the run. She sniffed about, picked up a piece of bread, dropped it again, sniffed at the meat, then to my relief began taking pieces of meat over to the wall to eat, furtive in every movement. I hoped then she would be all right.

My plan was to leave her in the kitchen for a few days, so that she could get used to Moobli and myself, then to take her for walks round the 'territory' on a collar and lead. I wanted her to run free around the cottage like a dog, but if she ran away the hounds would almost certainly get her if they returned this way. In due course she could have as her main home one of the old wildcat pens which Liane seldom used now.

Over the next few days I attempted to tame Aspen. Once she scrambled up the chimney and stayed on a ledge. As I tried to lift her down she bit my hand but not hard enough to pierce the skin. I soothed her, wiped her clean and by constant stroking, talking gently, caressing her, *showing* human love to her in the way I had tamed the wildcat Liane as a kitten, attempted to gain her trust. I wanted her to feel that love. When she was hungry or thirsty, I held food or milk out to her so that she had to come forward to take them, had to come close of her own free will.

She liked being held upside down on my lap and having her tummy tickled. Her eyes would half close and twinkle then, and she made frothy bubbles in her mouth. If I sat down with legs straight out, she would come forward furtively and nibble my boots, her eyes never leaving my face. She watched a rolling ball with interest, touched it with her nose but never picked it up like a dog. When I held out rolled-up newspaper, she sniffed it, then seized it in her teeth and began to pull. She came to like, and expect, a tug-of-war every day. Once she vanished behind the far slab leg of my kitchen table, then shyly peeped out to see if I was still there. Slowly I slid behind the other leg and peeped out at her in exactly the same way. When I slid back, she peeped out again, wanting to know where I had gone. When I emerged she dodged behind her slab again. This became a regular game of hide and seek.

On the fifth day I put a broad leather collar and long lead on her and took her outside. Immediately she bounced about

like a hare, pulling with exceptional strength for an animal her
size, and tried to burrow through and between grasses, rushes
and brambles. While it was fine exercise, making her strong,
it was arousing her wild instincts too early and I kept her in the
kitchen a few more days.

Sometimes, if she fed well, she would eat nothing the next
day. This must happen in the wild, especially if the parents do
not find food. Once, when I found a mouse Liane had caught,
I tied nylon line round its neck and jerked it about but Aspen
would not chase it. When I removed the line, however, she ate
it fast. Soon she took to burrowing. She dug her way under the
hearth, tearing away sticks and logs with surprising strength.
Then it was difficult to get her out, even by tugging her collar,
as her large head kept getting stuck, but she remained passive
as I cleaned her up. I did not wash her with water, for fear she
might catch cold, but blew out the dust and ashes, while comb-
ing the fur. She burrowed under papers, and the cardboard
covering a gap under my old cooker, tearing away with both
front feet like a furious boxer, looking round every now and
again to see if I, danger, was still there. She picked up wads
of paper in her mouth and shook them like a little dog.

When I next took Aspen out, she again ran to the end of the
long rope and bounded up and down like a little kangaroo,
pausing to look at me now and again. Afterwards she sat down
with open mouth panting, showing her long pink tongue. I
noticed she yawned a lot when puzzled or unsure what to do.
I sat down and kept still a long time. Slowly she crept forward,
keeping low in the grass, sniffed at my boots, then jerked her
head back as if she had been stung. After that she kept sitting
down, but not at the end of the tether, and gradually I hauled
in the slack until she was only two feet away. Moving slowly,
I lifted her on to my lap, stroked her soft head where it lay
draped over one knee, and then let go of her. She stayed there
for a while, not realising she was free. When she did, she
bounded away again. She felt scared sometimes when I picked
her up; her ears went back, though not as far as a wildcat's, and

she opened her mouth, but she made no sound, nor did she bite. I also noticed that she did not like mutton. She would just give it a nip or two before dropping it. She greedily ate minced beef or ox hearts but not lamb flank, the cheapest cut of all. Here was a fox that actually disliked sheep meat! She only ate it if there was nothing else. Sometimes she covered meat up with hay, pushing it over with her nose, as if keeping a food cache. She had little body odour; nor did her droppings smell strongly. Usually she urinated on a sawdust pile provided for the purpose. She was easier to house-train than any of the wild-cats were as kittens.

One evening I brought her into my study-bedroom. She was immediately curious about the new surroundings, looking at the desk, the bed, the things on the bed, the ceiling, always with sly glances back at me. If she headed for dark places a slight tug on the line made her sit down with a flump. Next evening I took in Moobli too, telling him not to hurt her, for they would have to become friends if she was to run free about the place one day. Good as gold he sat down, but when his head went near, to sniff her, her ears went back, she glared and made a weak '*bic*' spit at him, snapping her jaws. Moobli whined with a hurt look on his face and withdrew his head again. Once she jumped on to the bed and stretched upwards, seeming all long legs, and when she craned her neck over its edge, her tail straight out behind, her body elongated so she looked like a beautiful long slim arrow. I put her on my desk. When I stopped stroking her she crept over the desk top and jumped into a box of soft files. She found it a natural cup and lay look-ing at me for over an hour as I typed, her head resting on its rim. Every time I looked up it was to see her sleepy eyes gazing into mine. She would now take meat from my hand, approach-ing gingerly to snap it up, then backing up to eat it a few feet away.

The next time I brought Aspen into the study she charged about, scraped the firewood logs over the floor and dug up the carpet. She even tried to burrow through the concrete floor, her

rear legs wide apart through which to throw the earth — if there
had been any. This time, when I brought Moobli in, her
reaction was different. She stretched her neck curiously,
wandered towards him, ready to flee at a split second's notice.
When he extended his nose to greet hers she opened her mouth
like a great long beak and tried to nip his lip. Knowing I wanted
him to accept her, Moobli just moved his head out of the way.
Later, when he was lying near the bed and she was under it,
she sneaked up to him and sniffed the whole length of his body.
It was then she seemed to decide that he was not just a big fox
dog but a *dog*, and all her wild instincts came up. She actually
went to attack the giant, barked at his swiftly withdrawn head,
then tried to nip his feet and jaw, but Moobli drew his feet in
and dodged her easily.

It was interesting to see that once she found he was passive,
instead of thinking of him as a kind and harmless animal, she
went on the attack, assaulting weakness, taking the predator's
rôle. The fact that he could have ended her life with one swift
chop apparently escaped her mind once she felt sure he would
not assault her. She soon tired of that game, however, and lay
with her head on her paws, which were turned outwards, looking first at Moobli and then back at me, as if trying to work
out why two such traditional enemies were being so friendly.

I was now sure that Moobli would not hurt her and began
to leave her outside on a rope tied to the bird table, so that she
could run fifteen yards in any direction. She was still scared of
Moobli, yet was also intensely fascinated by him, and nearly
always went up to him first. He began to play with her, running
up and down as she snapped at him, boxing her gently with his
paws and easily dodging her bites, which seemed to be made
without serious intent to inflict injury.

The Search

from *The Midnight Fox*

by Betsy Byars

Like a great many other characters in books, Tommy is unhappy at the thought of spending two months on his aunt Millie's farm while his parents are away. Sure enough for the first few days he is bored stiff, and missing his friend Petie. But when he sees a black fox leaping gracefully over the crest of a field nearby he becomes filled with desire to see her again. Hazeline is his cousin, Mr Hunter a neighbouring farmer.

Black foxes, incidentally, are not a special variety but an accident of nature — perhaps one cub in a litter will happen to be that colour.

For the past two weeks I had been practically tearing the woods apart looking for the den of the black fox. I had poked under rocks and logs and stuck sticks in rotted trees, and it was a wonder that some animal had not come storming out and just bitten my hand off.

I had found a hornet's nest like a huge grey shield in a tree. I had found a bird's nest, low in a bush, with five pale-blue eggs and no mother to hatch them. I had found seven places where chipmunks lived. I had found a brown owl who never moved from one certain limb of one certain tree. I had heard a tree, split by lightning years ago, suddenly topple and crash to the ground, and I ran and got there in time to see a disgruntled possum run down the broken tree and into the woods. But I did not find the place where the black fox lived.

Now, on this day, I did not go into the woods at all. I had gone up the creek where there was an old chimney, all that was left of somebody's cabin. I had asked Aunt Millie about it, but all she could remember was that some people named Bowden had worked on the farm a long time ago and had lived here. I poked around the old chimney for a while because I was hoping I would find something that had belonged to the Bowdens, and then I gave that up and walked around the bend.

I sat on a rock, perfectly still, for a long time and looked down into the creek. There were crayfish in the water — I could see them, sometimes partly hidden beneath a covering of sand, or I could see the tips of their claws at the edge of a rock. There were fish in the water so small I could almost see through them. They stayed right together, these fish, and they moved together too.

After a while I looked across the creek and I saw a hollow where there was a small clearing. There was an outcropping of rocks behind the clearing and an old log slanted against the rocks. Soft grass sloped down to the creek bank.

I don't know how long I sat there — I usually forgot about my watch when I was in the woods — but it was a long time. I was just sitting, not expecting anything or waiting for anything. And the black fox came through the bushes.

She set a bird she was carrying on the ground and gave a small yapping bark, and at once, out of a hole beneath the rocks came a baby fox.

He did not look like his mother at all. He was tiny and woolly and he had a stubby nose. He stumbled out of the hole and fell on the bird as if he had not eaten in a month. I have never seen a fiercer fight in my life than the one that baby fox gave that dead bird. He shook it, pulled it, dragged it this way and that, all the while growling and looking about to see if anyone or anything was after his prize.

The black fox sat watching with an expression of great satisfaction. Mothers in a park sometimes watch their young children with this same fond, pleased expression. Her eyes were golden and very bright as she watched the tiny fox fall over the bird, rise, and shake it.

In his frenzy he dropped the bird, picked up an older dried bird wing in its place, and ran around the clearing. Then, realizing his mistake, he returned and began to shake the bird with even greater fierceness. After a bit he made another mistake, dropping the bird by his mother's tail, and then trying to run off with that.

In the midst of all this, there was a noise. It was on the other side of the clearing, but the black fox froze. She made a faint sound, and at once the baby fox, still carrying his bird, disappeared into the den.

The black fox moved back into the underbrush and waited. I could not see her but I knew she was waiting to lead the danger, if there was any, away from her baby. After a while I heard her bark from the woods, and I got up quietly and moved back down the creek. I did not want the black fox to see me and know that I had discovered her den. Hazeline had told me that foxes will pick up their young like cats and take them away if they think someone has discovered their den.

I wondered if this was how the black fox had come to have only one baby. Perhaps her den had been the one discovered by Mr Hunter. Perhaps she had started to move her cubs and only got one to safety before Mr Hunter had arrived with his dynamite.

I decided I would never come back here to bother her. I knew I would be tempted, because already I wanted to see that fox play with his bird some more, but I would not do it. If I was to see the black fox again, it would be in the woods, or in the pasture, or in the ravine, but I was not going to come to the den ever again. I did not know that an awful thing was going to happen which would cause me to break this resolution.

The Vixen

by John Clare

Among the taller wood with ivy hung,
The old fox plays and dances round her young.
She snuffs and barks if any passes by
And swings her tail and turns prepared to fly.
The horseman hurries by, she bolts to see,
And turns agen, from danger never free.
If any stands she runs among the poles
And barks and snaps and drives them in their holes.
The shepherd sees them and the boy goes by
And gets a stick and progs the hole to try.
They get all still and lie in safety sure,
And out again when everything's secure,
And start and snap at blackbirds bouncing by
To fight and catch the great white butterfly.

When spots of rain fall and the sun is shining, a fox is getting
married.

Old folk saying

The Shelter

from *A Family of Foxes*

by Eilis Dillon

'They say that foxes can turn themselves into men and women . . . They say they are witches that get themselves up like animals . . .' This is the sort of superstition that Colm and his friends Patsy, Séamus and Michael hear from the adults on the island off the west coast of Ireland where they live. Then the boys rescue two half-drowned foxes from the sea — they are silver foxes, whose fur has white touches giving it a silvery appearance. Mr Thornton is their kind and enlightened schoolteacher.

For a few minutes the boys sat perfectly still, watching how the foxes' ribs went up and down slowly, with a little shiver in between. Their eyes were opening every moment and their ears were beginning to twitch.

'The salt water is tickling their skin,' Patsy said.

At that moment the bigger fox sat up and began to lick himself like a dog.

'He'll have a thirst on him after all that salt,' said Michael. 'Wherever we bring him, there must be water handy'.

'Wherever we bring them, there must be a stone floor,' said Séamus. 'Foxes are a fright to burrow.'

They were silent again while they thought, trying to remember everything they had ever heard about the habits of foxes, and how to look after them. After a few mintues Colm said:

'I've been thinking hard, and I can say truly that I never in all my life heard a good word for a fox. All I ever heard was how to shoot them or trap them. They were telling a story in our house about a fox that saw the trap that was laid for him and didn't he drop a rock on it to make it go off. Then he rolled on the ground and laughed and laughed, and went into his burrow. But the men had been watching and they laid two traps the next time. The fox dropped a stone into the first trap, but when he rolled on the ground and laughed, didn't he roll into the second trap so that it snapped and caught him. In all the stories it's the same thing — they always catch the fox in the end.'

' 'Tis true,' said Patsy. 'We must hide them very well. I wish we could bring them to another island.'

The others disagreed with this.

'Where would you bring them where they'd be safe? The men go hunting on all the islands.'

'How could we bring them food on another island? We'd surely be seen, going and coming.'

'Some days we couldn't go and come at all, if the weather was bad.'

'Some days we wouldn't be allowed in the currachs.'

'If they were on another island we'd never have a right chance to play with them,' said Colm, who was stroking the smaller fox's head. 'Think of it this way: where would the foxes like to be?'

'A wild place.'

'A safe place.'

'A dry place.'

'A place where there would be no red foxes around,' said Patsy. 'If these are foxes, they are not like the red ones. The red ones mightn't like them, the way red cows don't like black and white cows. 'Twould be as bad if the red foxes were to kill them as if the men were to do it.'

'The red foxes! Would they do that?'

'They have a bad reputation,' Patsy said. 'I wouldn't put it past them.'

'A safe place will be hard to find,' said Michael. 'And we haven't much time to find it. As soon as they are rested, they'll likely get up and run off, and we'd have no chance in the world of catching them. Do you know that shelter for sheep, down by Casla?'

'The one that belongs to Morty Quinn?'

'Yes, yes, that's the one. Morty hasn't owned a sheep for years. He never goes down there. He told me himself that he's afraid of breaking his leg. Old people are queer — they do be all afraid of breaking their leg.'

'I know the way in,' said Séamus. 'There's ferns as high as your head and brambles and thick, thick grass, all squeezed in between two little stone walls.'

'That's the place. We'll have a job getting in there ourselves.'

'We can walk along the tops of the walls. That's something old Morty couldn't do.'

'Maybe if it's such a fine place for foxes, there will be a few red ones living there already.'

They all shivered at the thought of the red ones, but they agreed that this would not stop them from going there.

By now, the smaller fox had begun to sit up too, and to lick herself in a tired way. The bigger one watched her with his ears cocked. For a moment, the boys wondered if he would allow himself to be lifted up, but he didn't struggle at all. He seemed to have got heavier since they laid him on the grass. Patsy and Colm took the bigger one between them, and Michael and Séamus took the smaller one.

'It's a pity we can't take them on the donkey-cart,' Patsy said. 'Even a piece of the way would be a help.'

But this was impossible. The donkey-cart could only go on the road, and the only road ran right between the houses.

'I can imagine all the old ones coming out to the doors to watch us, and see what we have on the cart,' Patsy said. 'That wouldn't be a secret for long.'

'Can't we take the ass without the cart?' said Colm.

This seemed a good idea at first sight, but when they came close to the donkey, carrying the foxes, he made it quite clear that he hated them. He pranced about and brayed and tossed his head in the air, backing the cart as hard as he could against the stones.

'It's queer how he doesn't like them,' Colm said uneasily. 'He'd never stand them lying across his back, that's certain.'

' 'Tis the smell, I suppose,' Michael said. 'I can hardly stand it myself.'

' 'Tis no worse than bad fish, or the shark that was washed up by the tide,' Colm said indignantly.

'I could hardly stand them either,' said Michael. 'Come on, while we have time, we'd better shorten the road.'

It was true that a strong smell, of a kind that they had never smelt before, came from the foxes. Since their fur had partly dried it had become more pungent, and as Michael said, only that a strong wind was blowing, they would never have been able to endure it.

'It's well they're not struggling,' said Séamus. 'This way we can go faster.'

They went along the top of the shore, where the stones were round and smooth from the winter storms. With the extra weight of the foxes, their feet were soon tired and sore, and they had to sit down often and rest. Each time that they did this, they were afraid that the moment the foxes would find themselves on the ground, they would spring up and run off. But they made no move. They just lay there quite slack and still.

'Perhaps they're sick,' Colm said suddenly, and he began to cry. 'Perhaps they're going to die. When we reach Morty Quinn's shed, perhaps we'll have only two dead foxes.'

He hugged the one he was carrying. It put out a long, slow, pink tongue and licked his ear.

'Look at that!' said Patsy. 'If that fellow was near his death, he'd never be bothered with licking your ear. Stop howling now, or you'll bring down the whole island on top of us.'

Colm put his ear to the fox's mouth, to have it licked again.
He stopped wailing, quite suddenly, and said:

'I know what's wrong with them, of course. They're hungry.
We don't know how long they're in the water — it could be
hours. It could even be a few days! That's what it is: they're
hungry!'

And he began to rummage in his pocket with one hand, grip-
ping his part of the fox with the other. He fished out a crust
of bread, a bit grey but still quite good. Very gently he put it
against the fox's mouth. The fox sniffed it once or twice, and
then opened its mouth and snapped the whole piece, chewed
it frantically and swallowed it. Then it began to push at Colm
with its nose.

'That's it, of course,' they all said, and they rummaged until,
they found crusts in their own pockets.

They divided them fairly between the two, but they could see
that what they had was only like a crumb to them.

'Let's get them to the shelter first,' Michael said after a
minute. 'That will give us time to think, at least.'

They followed the line of the shore until they came to a long
spur of land running out into the sea. Halfway along this spur
was the shelter that belonged to Morty Quinn. It was no
wonder that he no longer used it. The land was low here, and
in winter-time the salt sea spray drifted over it, sometimes for
weeks together if the sea was stormy. Now in the spring it would
be quite a healthy place for the foxes, the boys thought. The
grass was already long, because it had been a warm, sunny
spring, and when they looked across at it from the shore, it
looked green and fresh and bright.

The nearest house to the shelter was half a mile away. It was
Mr Thornton's house, which was a good thing because, being
a stranger, he was not so much interested in the activities of his
neighbours. When the island people were gossiping at their
doors, Mr Thornton preferred to be inside by the fire reading
one of his books.

'Our foxes couldn't have a better neighbour,' Patsy said.

Fox Dancing

by Suzanne Knowles

Tall as a foxglove spire, on tiptoe
The fox in the wilderness dances;
His pelt and burnished claws reflect
The sun's and the moon's glances.

From blackberry nose to pride of tail
He is elegant, he is gay;
With his pawsteps as a pattern of joy
He transfigures the day.

For a hat he wears a rhubarb leaf
To keep his thinking cool,
Through which his fur-lined ears prick up.
This fox, he is no fool

And does not give a good-morning
For the condition of his soul:
With the fox dancing in the desert
Study to be whole.

Fox in a Bookshop

from *For Love of a Wild Thing*

by Ernest Dudley

*Ernest Dudley's book, which describes the rearing and training of the fox
Rufus, is set mainly in Scotland, but the extract here takes place in a bookshop. So tame had Rufus become, although he still lived in the wild, that
he was due to appear in a film, and the author brought Rufus down to
London to see the producer. He had written a first book about Rufus,
and it was at the time of publication of this in paperback that there were
'bookshop signings' by Rufus as part of a publicity tour.*

Wherever he went, whoever he met, on his tours of children's
hospital-wards, bookshops, television stations — wheverever it
was — after the initial astonishment at the sight of a wild fox
who could behave like Rufus, not only did he receive the V.I.P.
treatment, he was always accepted as a friend. A sort of friend
of the family, you could say, whom you could trust — you knew
he would never let you down, he would be at the bookshop, paw
ready to sign his 'autograph', on time; at the television studio
on time. Everyone, from shop-assistants to tea-girls, make-up
girls (not that he ever needed make-up, but everyone of the
studio staff crowded round to watch him when the show went

out), to the interviewer, took him to their hearts at once. When he left there remained an unforgettable memory of a wonderfully loving creature. It was the same at every pub to which we would adjourn with the media men and women, every hotel or restaurant — he would sit down quietly beside Don, roll on his back for a good scratch, or give an occasional yawn if he felt that perhaps it was time we should be moving on.

It wasn't as if you were with a fox or any other animal, it was more like being with another human being, a warm, loving human being who was there alongside, happy to do all he could to cooperate, however best he could. It was only in the studio, when there was the inevitable wait while everything was being set up for his interview, that he became a little bad-mannered. The lights would become unbearably hot and he used to start to stick out his tongue and pant a bit, and then there would be a rush to find him a bowl of water — champagne or the hard stuff was not allowed so soon before transmission, as the possibility of his uttering a hiccup wasn't thought to be good for his image — and in his haste to get at the water he might upset the bowl, which gave him the idea of racing round the studio with it in his teeth. Apart from an occasional lapse of this sort, there was never any fit of temperament, he chattered and showed his teeth in his happy 'grin' on cue; he was the perfect television interviewee.

It was the same today. After breakfast, in which he didn't join — his one-meal-only-at-night routine never varied — we were whisked off to the book-show, where publishers, media people, photographers, and children, some with their parents, some in parties with their teachers, took him, literally, to their bosoms. He disappeared from sight to the accompaniment of the usual oohing and aahing, squeals of disbelieving enchantment and then the roar of joyful admiration. At last, Don and I between us, aided by the publishers, who were alarmed in case something awful happened to him, managed to 'rescue' Rufus and get him going on the serious business of gracefully yielding to autograph-hunters' requests, hundreds of them waving their

Rufus books — some bought on the spot, others which had been brought along. Untiringly Rufus stuck his paw on the ink-pad, then placed it on the page. Ink-pad . . . book. Ink-pad . . . book. Ink-pad . . . book. And the cameras popped. And the small boy, school-cap knocked awry over one ear by Rufus, to whom he held on as if he would never let him go, begging: 'Can I keep him? Please let me — he doesn't bark all the time, like my dog. You can have my dog in exchange—'

Fox

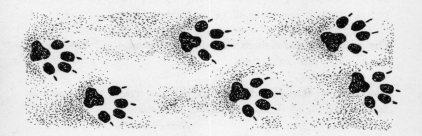

by Laurence Smith

Sun plushed eve
and mauve the chilly air
Ice brittle grass squeaks
and creaks as the lone
fox
trips his slinky way
along the inky hedge
He barks and splits the misty air with his
gasping yell.

Acknowledgements

The editor and publishers would like to thank the following for use of copyright material:

Extract from Rosalind Kerven's *Who Ever Heard of a Vegetarian Fox?*: reproduced with permission of Blackie & Son Ltd.

Extract from Roald Dahl's *Fantastic Mr Fox*: reproduced with permission of Murray Pollinger, Literary Agent, published by HarperCollins Publishers and Penguin Books Ltd.

Extract from Brian Morse's *Sauce for the Fox*: reproduced with permission of Hodder & Stoughton Ltd.

Charles Causley's poem 'A Fox Came Into My Garden' is from *Figgie Hobbin*, published by Macmillan.

Extract from Michael Morpurgo's *Little Foxes*: published by Octopus Children's Books.

Extract from Antonia Forest's *Peter's Room*: published by Faber & Faber Ltd.

'A Little Vixen': © Marcus Crouch 1989. Reprinted from *Ivan: Stories of Old Russia* by Marcus Crouch (1989) by permission of Oxford University Press.

Extract from John Masefield's *Reynard the Fox*: reproduced with permission of the Society of Authors as the literary representative of the Estate of John Masefield.

Extract from William Corlett's *The Steps Up the Chimney*: published by Bodley Head (1990).

Extracts from Colin Dann's *Fox's Feud* and *The Fox Cub Bold:* published by Hutchinson.

Extract from *Free Spirit* by Michael Chambers: reprinted by permission of Methuen London.

Extract from *Red Fox* by Charles G. D. Roberts: Copyright © 1905 and renewal copyright © 1933 by Charles G. D. Roberts. Reprinted by permission of Farrar, Straus & Giroux Inc.

Stanley Cook's poem 'The Fox Who Came to Town': © 1981, from *Fox Poems*, ed. John Foster (Oxford University Press, 1991).

Lew Sarett's poem 'Four Little Foxes': from *Slow Smoke* © 1953 by Lew Sarett. Used by permission of Lloyd Sarett Stockdale.

Extract from *Out of the Wild* by Mike Tomkies: published by Jonathan Cape.

Extract from *The Midnight Fox* by Betsy Byars: published by Faber & Faber Ltd.

Extract from *A Family of Foxes* by Eilis Dillon: published by Faber & Faber Ltd, and reproduced by permission of David Bolt Associates.

Suzanne Knowles' poem 'Fox Dancing' is from *The Sea Bell and Other Poems*, published by J M Dent & Sons Ltd.

Extract from *For Love of a Wild Thing* by Ernest Dudley: published by Frederick Muller.

Laurence Smith's poem 'Fox' is from *Catch the Light* (Oxford University Press, 1982).

Index of Authors

Index of Titles

Index of Sources

Other great reads ⟍*from* **Red Fox**

Further Red Fox titles that you might enjoy reading are listed on the following pages. They are available in bookshops or they can be ordered directly from us.

If you would like to order books, please send this form and the money due to:

ARROW BOOKS, BOOKSERVICE BY POST, PO BOX 29, DOUGLAS, ISLE OF MAN, BRITISH ISLES. Please enclose a cheque or postal order made out to Arrow Books Ltd for the amount due, plus 30p per book for postage and packing to a maximum of £3.00, both for orders within the UK. For customers outside the UK, please allow 35p per book.

NAME _____

ADDRESS _____

_____

Please print clearly.

Whilst every effort is made to keep prices low, it is sometimes necessary to increase cover prices at short notice. If you are ordering books by post, to save delay it is advisable to phone to confirm the correct price. The number to ring is THE SALES DEPARTMENT 071 (if outside London) 973 9700.

Other great reads from **Red Fox**

Animal stories from Enid Blyton

If you like reading stories about animals, you'll love Enid Blyton's animal books.

THE BIRTHDAY KITTEN

Terry and Tessie want a pet for their birthday – but when the big day comes, they're disappointed.

ISBN 0 09 924100 5   £1.99

THE BIRTHDAY KITTEN and
THE BOY WHO WANTED A DOG

A great value two-books-in-one containing two stories about children and their lovable pets.

ISBN 0 09 977930 7   £2.50

HEDGEROW TALES

Go on a journey through the woodlands and fields and meet the fascinating animals who live there.

ISBN 0 09 980880 3   £2.50

MORE HEDGEROW TALES

A second set of animal stories packed with accurate details.

ISBN 0 09 980880 3   £2.50

THE ADVENTURES OF SCAMP

Scamp the puppy is nothing but a bundle of mischief – and he does get into a lot of trouble.

ISBN 0 09 987860 7   £2.99

Other great reads from **Red Fox**

Discover the Red Fox poetry collections

CADBURY'S NINTH BOOK OF CHILDREN'S POETRY
Poems by children aged 4–16.
ISBN 0 09 983450 2 £4.99

THE COMPLETE SCHOOL VERSE
ed. Jennifer Curry
Two books in one all about school.
ISBN 0 09 991790 4 £2.99

MY NAME, MY POEM ed. Jennifer Curry
Find *your* name in this book.
ISBN 0 09 948030 1 £1.95

MONSTROSITIES Charles Fuge
Grim, gruesome poems about monsters.
ISBN 0 09 967330 4 £3.50

LOVE SHOUTS AND WHISPERS Vernon Scannell
Read about all sorts of love in this book.
ISBN 0 09 973950 X £2.99

CATERPILLAR STEW Gavin Ewart
A collection describing all sorts of unusual animals.
ISBN 0 09 967280 4 £2.50

HYSTERICALLY HISTORICAL Gordon Snell and Wendy Shea
Madcap rhymes from olden times
ISBN 0 09 972160 0 £2.99

Other great reads from **Red Fox**

Discover the great animal stories of Colin Dann

JUST NUFFIN

The Summer holidays loomed ahead with nothing to look forward to except one dreary week in a caravan with only Mum and Dad for company. Roger was sure he'd be bored.

But then Dad finds Nuffin: an abandoned puppy who's more a bundle of skin and bones than a dog. Roger's holiday is transformed and he and Nuffin are inseparable. But Dad is adamant that Nuffin must find a new home. Is there *any* way Roger can persuade him to change his mind?

ISBN 0 09 966900 5   £2.99

KING OF THE VAGABONDS

'You're very young,' Sammy's mother said, 'so heed my advice. Don't go into Quartermile Field.'

His mother and sister are happily domesticated but Sammy, the tabby cat, feels different. They are content with their lot, never wondering what lies beyond their immediate surroundings. But Sammy is burningly curious and his life seems full of mysteries. Who is his father? Where has he gone? And what is the mystery of Quartermile Field?

ISBN 0 09 957190 0   £2.99